TRANSIENT

By
WARD MOORE

I0616791

ARMCHAIR FICTION
PO Box 4369, Medford, Oregon 97504

IMAGINE A FANTASTIC NIGHTMARE THAT'S REAL...

This is one of the most unusual novels you will find in the entire Armchair Fiction product line. It is an insightful, often dark fantasy laced with chimerical imagery and morbid imagination.
A man of political clout with a reputation to uphold finds himself lost in an obscure landscape full of confusion and distorted reality.

Within these pages is an account of one man's truly weird and grim existence. Rape, suicide, fantasy, delusional thinking, twisted and sickening romance…all this goes together in a penetrating but disturbingly uncomfortable narrative of one man's off centered thinking.

FOR A SECOND COMPLETE NOVEL, TURN TO PAGE 123

ABOUT WARD MOORE

Ward Moore...

...was born in Madison, New Jersey, August 10, 1903. Popular rumor had it that Moore was expelled from High School for anti war activity during World War I, but Moore claimed he quit school in order to start writing. He also claimed to have spent several years as a hobo, traveling around the country until he ended up in Chicago where he met renowned poet Kenneth Rexroth.

Moore's most famous story is "Bring the Jubilee." In this notable work the South wins the American Civil War. The main character is doomed to live in this alternate reality with no way "home" because his time machine, which was borne of the North's win, cannot be re-invented.

Moore was not known to conform to any one genre of writing and many of his stories are written as if intended for his enjoyment only.

He died in 1978 in Pacific Grove, CA.

CHAPTER ONE

THE Governor, a widower in his earliest fifties, turned off the ignition, noting with satisfaction the absence of street signs limiting parking time. Governor Lampley, serving out the unexpired term of his predecessor and not entirely hopeless of nomination and election in his own right, pictured the stupid or fanatical cop who under any circumstances would write a ticket for the car with the license GOV-001. He and Marvin had made a big joke out of those zeros, Marvin showing his hostility under the kidding, the Governor hiding his dislike for his secretary under his self-deprecation.

Before getting out he dusted the knees of his trousers and looked up and down the shabby street. The Odd Fellows Hall was built of concrete blocks; Almon Lampley was reasonably sure it hadn't been there thirty years before. The other buildings seemed to be as he remembered them, if anything so fragile as the reconstruction in his mind could be called a memory. He'd forgotten the name of the place, its very location. Only the highway marker, the one so close it rooted the town briefly from obscurity to pinpoint it fleetingly: so many miles from the capital behind him, so many miles to the destination before him, hit the chord. Why, it was here. This was the place. How very long, long ago. Goodness (he curbed the natural profanity of even his thoughts lest he offend some straitlaced voter), goodness— years and years. A generation. Before he met Mattie, before he switched from selling agricultural implements to vote-getting.

And the sign just outside, Pop. 1,983. Pathetic lack of 17 more pop. With 2,000 they could have boasted: We're on our way, on our third thousand, the biggest little town between here and there. Watch us grow. If you lived here, you'd be home now. Get in on the ground floor and expand with us, Tomorrow's metropolis. Under two thousand was stagnation, decay, surrender. 1,983: possibly a thousand registered voters; more likely eight hundred—two precincts. How many Republicans, how many Democrats? Maybe three screwballs: one voting Prohibition, one writing in his own name, one casting a ballot for Pogo. A sad town, a dead town. Surely it hadn't been so thirty years ago?

But there had been the railroad then, and young Almon Lampley swinging down from the daycoach before the wheels stopped turning, bursting with enthusiasm, eager, cocky, invincible. The railroad gone, its tracks melted into scrap, its ties piled up and burned, its place taken by trucking lines, buses, cars. You had to have progress. So what if the town got lost in the process, fell behind? There were other towns, equally deserving, equally promising, equally anxious to get ahead. The state was full of them: chicory capital of the world, hub of mink breeding, where the juiciest pickles are made, home-owners' heaven, the friendliest city, Santa Claus' summer residence, host to the annual girly festival, gateway to the alkali flats. Thousands of them. And he was governor of the whole state. It would be non-feasance if not mis-feasance in him to regret this one bypassed settlement.

Evidently progress, before it withered, had brought the Odd Fellows Hall. No more. The false fronted stores were as he remembered—as he thought he ought to have remembered—and the dwelling set back from the street, forgotten or held in irascible obstinacy, petunias and geraniums growing too lush in the overgrown front yard. The Hay, Grain & Feed where he had called—where he must have called—the garage, the Chevrolet agency, the hotel.

The Governor gave a final brush to his trousers, pocketed the keys, and picked up his overnight case from the seat beside him.   The hotel was unquestionably the most prominent building on either side of the street yet he had unconsciously (unconsciously?) left noticing it to the last.   It was a square three stories high, probably older than anything else in town, of no identifiable style, with a sign saying glumly ROOMS, MEALS, in paint so ancient its surface had peeled away, leaving only fossil pigment to take the weather and continue the message.   The brown clapboards had grayed, they were parted—driven asunder—by a vertical column of match-fencing, mincingly precise in its senility, pierced by multi-paned windows with random blue, brown, green and yellow glass.   The verandah, empty of chairs but suggestive of a place for drummers to sit with their heels on the collapsing railing, sagged in a twisted list.   The two balconies above it had been mended with scrap lumber, unpainted, and the repairs themselves mended again.

Governor Lampley could easily have driven another thirty, forty, fifty miles—it was only mid-afternoon and he was not tired—to find modern accommodations.   He could have driven all the way to his destination.   He chose to stop here. As a sentimental gesture?   As an uncomfortable (fleas, lumpy beds, creaky floors) amusement?   As a whim?   Call it a whim. The Governor was on an unofficial, very limited, vacation.

He admitted feeling slightly foolish as he took the three steps to the verandah and walked over the uneasy boards to the plate-glass doors and into the darkened, dusty lobby.   In this position one didn't give way to sudden impulse.   Any yielding to sentiment was calculated, studied, designed to be milked for good publicity.   He could see the bored, competent photographers, the casual-well-planned-chat with the reporters.   Marvin would have arranged it all; the

Governor would have only to move gracefully through his part.

Responsibly he ought to phone Marvin, let him know he was staying here, give his attention to whatever business Marvin would say couldn't wait till tomorrow. In imagination he could hear the querulous, nagging tones beneath the surface respectfulness, the barely suppressed astonishment (what do you suppose he's up to now? a woman? a meeting with one of the doughboys? a drunk?), the assurance Marvin would call if anything came up. He ought to phone Marvin immediately.

The thought of Marvin made him turn and glance back through the doorway, to reassure himself he was not part of a scheduled program after all. But there was no car on the street save his own, no busy technicians, no curious onlookers, no one. Only the afternoon sunlight, the swirling motes, the faint smell of oil and dust.

As soon as he accustomed his eyes to the dimness he saw there was no one in the lobby. An artificial palm, its raffia swathing loose as a two year old's diaper, stood in a wooden tub. Eight chairs were placed in neatly opposing rows, four covered in once-black leather, cracked and split, the wrinkles worn brown, four wooden, humbly straight. There was an air of peacefulness independent of the dark, the quiet, the emptiness, an assertion that there was no need to hurry here, that there was never a need to hurry here.

He lifted his arm to look at his watch. The sweep-second hand was not revolving. He put the watch to his ear; there was no tick. He wound it, shook it; it didn't start. He slipped it off his wrist into his pocket, and loosened his necktie.

He stood in front of the brown counter whose top was shiny with the patina of leaning elbows. There was a bell with inverted triple chins and outpopping pimple, an open register turned indifferently toward him, a bank of empty pigeonholes. He picked up the chewed pen with the splayed nib, bronze-shiny where the ink had dried on it. He had to tip the black scum-crusty inkwell far over to moisten it. It scratch-scratched across the top line on the page, engraving his name but only staining the depressions here and there, mostly on the down strokes. Oddly, instead of the capital, he wrote down the city he had once lived in, the city where he got his first job.

After registering he hesitated over the bell. Instead of ringing it he picked up his bag and walked to the shadowed stairway. Up ahead he saw a low-watt bulb staring bleakly on the wall. The area around the globe was a grimy green, outside the magic circle the pervading dark brown was undisturbed. The carpet under his feet was threadbare and gritty; through his shoe soles he felt the lumps of resistant knots in the wood, and the nail heads raised by the wearing-down around them. He gazed ahead.

There was a landing halfway up, opening on a narrow hall. Light came through fogged windows set close together along one wall. The other was papered with circus posters, the brightly lithographed elephants and hippopotami faded almost to indiscernability, the creases burst open like scored chestnuts. The Governor hesitated, went on up.

At the second floor he turned left, noting how spacious this hall was in contrast to the one below, how comparatively bright and clean. Most of the doors were slightly ajar, not inviting perhaps, merely indicating they were receptive to a tenant.

From the outside there was nothing to choose between them yet he felt the choice was important. Further, it seemed to him that opening a door would commit him; he must choose without inspection. Thoughtfully he passed several. The one he finally entered opened on a large room with two tall windows. Thin, brittle curtains drooped palely from the rods. Two dressers, the high one bellying forward, the low one supporting a tilted metal-dull mirror, were thick with cheap varnish that wept long blob-ended tears. The double bed was made, the coverlet turned down, the lumpy pillows smooth and gray. On a whatnot in one corner a glass bell enclosed two wax figures, a bride and groom in wedding finery. The wax bride was wringing her waxen hands.

The Governor put his bag on the foot of the bed, took off his jacket, rolled up his sleeves, went to the sink. The faucets were black-spotted, green-flecked, with remnants of nickel-plating and long dark scratches. The basin was orange-brown and gray-white. He turned on the HOT.

There was a quick hiss and a slurp of thick, liquid rust. He tried the COLD. The slurp was the same but there was no hiss. He looked around the room again, saw the washstand. The knobbly-spouted pitcher stood in the center of the knobbly-rimmed bowl. The water appeared good despite the dust floating on top. He poured some in the basin and rinsed his face and hands.

As a small child he had been sure water was life. Once he sprinkled some on a dead bird, stiff and ruffled. He found a towel, hard and grainy, dried his hands, shrinking slightly from the contact. He took his comb from his jacket and ran it through his still thick hair, only lightly graying. It was a minor pride that his campaign pictures were always the latest, never one taken when he was much younger.

He became aware he was being watched and turned inquiringly toward the door. The man standing there wore heavy work shoes, blue denim pants, a denim jacket buttoned to his neck. His face was dark, his straight black hair long. His eyes slanted ever so little above his high cheek bones. He smiled at Lampley. "Everything OK?"

"Everything OK," said Lampley. "Except the plumbing."

The man nodded thoughtfully.

"Oh, the plumbing. It went out." He gestured vaguely with his hands, indicating leaks, stoppages, broken pipes, hopeless fittings, worn-out heaters. "So we put in washstands."

"I see. Maybe it would have been better to have it fixed."

The other shook a doubtful head. "This was change. Advance. Improvement. Maybe next we'll put a well in every room, with a rope and bucket reaching straight down. Plop! And then rrrrr, up she comes full and slopping over. Or artesians with the water bubbling up like a billiard ball on the end of a cue. That would be hard to beat, ay? Or perhaps wooden pipes from the rain gutters."

"I see," said Lampley. The plans didn't seem unreasonable. "You're the clerk?" he asked politely.

"Clerk is good as any. Everyone has lots to do."

"That's right. Well, thanks."

"Don't mention it."

Lampley rolled down his sleeves, refastened his cufflinks, put his jacket back on. "Can I get something to eat here?"

"Why not? Come on."

The Governor followed him into the hall, closing the door. He thought briefly of asking about telephoning since there was no phone in his room. Still it wasn't really necessary; Marvin could take care of everything. The clerk led him, not to the stairs he had come up, but in the opposite direction. Some of the partially open doors were painted in vivid colors and marked with symbols strange to Lampley.

The backstairs were narrower, steeper, darker; the Governor had a constant fear of overestimating the width of the treads and placing a searching foot upon insubstantial air. They came to the halfway landing but instead of the windowed hall with the circus posters, they entered a low room, low as a ship's cabin compressed between decks. Exposed beams held up the ceiling. A long plank table ran between two benches, a high ladderback chair at the head and foot. One of the benches was built into the battened wall.

On it a man with an infantile face and bulging forehead under coarse black hair crouched over the table guarding his food with tiny kangaroo arms. A stained and spotted napkin was tied around his neck like a bib. He slobbered and gurgled over a bowl of thick porridge, smearing it around his mouth, spilling on the napkin as he scooped the mess from the bowl.

At the head of the table an old man, white-haired, hook-nosed, chewed silently. On the outside bench was a middle-aged woman with sagging, placid features, and a girl in her teens. All looked Indian or Mexican except the idiot, none paid attention to their arrival.

The clerk sat down at the foot of the table. Lampley saw there was no place for him except on the bench next to the defective. He edged his way in, staying far as possible from him. The room was suddenly oppressive; he had the notion they must be near a furnace, a boiler, a dynamo. He took out his carefully folded handkerchief and wiped his forehead. The old man glanced at him sympathetically.

The young girl reached under the table and came up with a bright green crepe paper party favor. She extended it diffidently toward the Governor. Smiling, he took hold of the stiff cardboard strip inside the ruffle with his thumb and forefinger. She giggled, holding the other end; they pulled. The cracker popped, a red tissue paper phrygian cap fell out. She clapped her hands and motioned him to put it on. Slightly embarrassed, he complied.

She searched through the torn favor for the motto, unfolded it. She shook her head and handed it to him. He read, AN UNOPENED BOOK HAS NO PRINTING. She put a bowl of beans, cut-up chicken, and rice before him. "Thank you," he said.

"For nothing," she responded, shyly polite. Her young breasts pushed out against her white shirt. Her dark eyes looked into his before her long lashes fell. Her mouth was wide and supple. Lampley realized she was beautiful. He thought with pain of walking with her through knee-high grass and lying beside her under spreading trees.

He spooned up some of the food; it was overcooked and tasteless. It didn't matter. Between spoonfuls he looked furtively at the woman—he dared not let his eyes return to the girl—and thought he saw a resemblance to... To whom? The face was pleasant, ordinary, memorable neither for charm nor repulsiveness. It was a matter of professional pride, an occupational necessity for him to remember faces; he could not recall this one. It nagged at the back of his mind.

The old man rose, wiping his mouth with the back of his hand, bowing clumsily toward the Governor. He pulled a wrinkled pack of cigarettes from his shirt pocket and extended it. "Thanks," acknowledged Lampley, "I don't use them." The old man shook his head, tipped the pack to his mouth, replaced it, lit the cigarette with a match struck on the seat of his trousers. His fingers were thick and twisted; they still appeared capable of delicate manipulation.

The clerk pushed back his chair. "We might put self-service in here," he remarked to one in particular. "Individual stoves, maybe mechanized farms or hydroponic tanks." He belched, holding his hand diffidently before his mouth.

Lampley emptied his bowl. The girl looked questioningly at him. "No more," he said. "Thank you."

She smiled at him, followed the clerk and the old man from the room; he was alone with the woman and the idiot. He wanted to get up and go too; something held him. "A long time," said the woman gently.

He knew what she meant; he refused to accept understanding. "I'm sorry."

"Since you were here. You forgot?"

There was coldness in his stomach. "No...not exactly. I'm sorry."

She shrugged. Her arms and shoulders were rounded and graceful but their grace did not obscure the fact that she was old as he, or nearly. Why was it so reprehensible to long for freshness and beauty in women but the stamp of taste to want these qualities in anything else? "I'm sorry," he said for the third time, aware of the phrase's futility.

She smiled, showing a gold tooth. The others were white but uneven. "For nothing," she echoed the girl. "What is there to be sorry for?"

His eyes went from the creature on the bench to her and back again.

"Yours," she said calmly.

He had known, but knowing and knowing were different things. "Impossible!"

She showed the gold tooth again. "Why impossible? You make love, you have babies."

"But—like that?"

"Does everything have to be perfect for you?"

He regarded her with greater horror than he had his—his son. A beast, an animal, giving birth to beasts and animals. "Not perfect. But not...this."

She laughed and moved around the table to the unfortunate. She untied the napkin and tenderly wiped his vacant face and the undeveloped hands. She kissed him passionately on the forehead. "You think it is possible to love only perfection? You couldn't love one like this, or an old woman, or a corpse?"

Lampley ran from the room, past a curtained entrance, and stumbled through a hall lit with yellow, grease-filmed light. The hall smelled of food, acrid, sickening. There was a swinging door at the end, padded, outlined with brass nails. Many were missing, their absence commemorated by the dark outline of where they had been. He pushed through it.

The kitchen was oddly constructed. Its ceiling seemed to be two stories high; just under it were niches for sooty plaster figures, all horribly distorted, figures with one arm twice the length of the other, phalluses long as legs, monstrous heads, steatophyrgian buttocks, goiters resting on sagittarian knees. Through a rose window yellow-pink beams streamed to the flagged floor. Scrubbed and sanded butchers' blocks splattered with gobs of fat, drying entrails, scabs of hard blood stood against the wall. Gleaming knives and cleavers were racked in the sides of the blocks. Tomb-like ranges were hooded in a row; opposite them empty spits turned before cold, blackened fireplaces.

The old man was seated on a stool before a slanting table, methodically chopping onions in a wooden bowl. He turned his head. "She gave you a hard time, hay?"

Blackmail, extortion, exposure, disgrace. "I don't know."

The old man wrinkled his forehead. The peculiar light made the creases unnaturally deep, like well-healed scars, "Who does know?" He laid down his cleaver. "Come."

Will-less, the Governor followed. The old man had a limp, formerly unnoticed. They went past the ranges to a massive steel door with a red lamp beside it. The old man lifted the tight latch. Lampley noted a safety device preventing the door from fully closing except from the outside.

They were in a large refrigerator. Sides of beef, barred red and pale, hung from hooks. Whole sheep and pigs, encased in stiff, unarmoring fat, thrust dead forefeet toward the unattainable sawdust-covered floor. Barrels of pickling brine, boxes of fish and seafood (the lobsters waving feelers uncertainly) were arranged neatly. It was cold; the Governor shivered. Plucked fowl dangled in rows. Beyond them wild ducks and geese, still sadly feathered, were suspended in bunches, three ducks, two geese to a bunch. The Governor touched a mallard's breast as he passed; the down was strangely warm in this chilling place.

They crossed an empty space. The whole carcass of an animal hung from gray hooks curving through the tendons of its legs. It had been skinned and gutted but the head was intact and untouched. The shaggy hair drooped forward, the horns pointed at nothing. The glazed eyes absorbed the light, the tongue, clenched between dead teeth, protruded.

"Buffalo," cried the Governor. "Surely it's against the law to kill them?"

The old man ran his dark, heavily veined hand gloatingly over the bison's hump and down the shoulder. "Tasty. Very tasty."

"You can't do things like this," insisted the Governor.

"Ah," sighed the old man. "Boom boom."

Lampley came closer. There were no signs of the buffalo having been shot. Its throat was cut and dark blood had congealed around the jagged wound. The old man picked out several clots of dried blood and put them in his mouth, sucking appreciatively. He rubbed his cheek against the head of the animal. "Soft," he said. "See yourself."

The Governor drew back.

The old man stared contemptuously at him. "No wonder."

16

"How do I get out of here?" asked Lampley.

The old man gestured indifferently. "Try that way." He waved his arm.

Lampley turned. Either the refrigerator had gotten colder or he was newly vulnerable to the chill. He shivered; hoarfrost crunched under his feet, the wall glistened with ice crystals. He realized he was not retracing his steps when he passed braces of partridges—or had he merely not noticed them before?—grouse, pheasants. He looked back; the old man was still nuzzling the bison head.

He came to a mound of snow and was puzzled, less at its presence than at its use and origin. Who would manufacture snow, and for what purpose? And if not manufactured it must have been brought a long way at great expense for it did not snow in this part of the state more than once in a dozen years.

But it was not a simple mound after all but an igloo, crudely constructed, as though by a child. Impulsively he got down on his knees and crawled through the entrance-tunnel until his head was inside. It was warm under the dome, warm and soothing and safe. He backed out quickly, frightened at the thought of becoming too content there, of not being able to leave its comfort.

The cold of the refrigerator was accentuated by the contrast; his breath came in steamy puffs. He hurried to a door opening from the inside. He leaned against the wall of a dark corridor and breathed deeply. The picture of the old man fondling the buffalo head was still before him. He felt his way slowly along the wall, and then he was in the lobby again. There was something wrong here: the room where they had eaten had been a half level higher.

There was no point in wondering over the layout of the hotel. He would retrieve his bag, get in the car and go on to his destination. He stumbled through the gloom, missing the stairs, and saw he was in front of an antique elevator, the doors open, the ancient basketwork cage an inch or two below the floor.

"Get in," invited the clerk. "I'll take you."

Lampley entered, panting a little, smoothing his tie with his palm. "Thank you."

The clerk pulled the grill shut; there was no door on the elevator itself. "Ninety-three million miles to the sun," he said. "We'd fry before we got there."

The Governor considered the idea. "Explode from lack of pressure, asphyxiate from lack of air first."

The clerk looked at him curiously. "We could shut our eyes and hold our breath, you know."

Lampley did not answer.

"All right." The clerk grasped the control lever. The cage fell with sickening velocity.

CHAPTER TWO

LAMPLEY knew something had broken but his fear was not absolute. He bent his knees (go limp: drunks and babies were less liable to injury than the stiffly erect); the drop would not be fatal, he might not even break a leg. How far to the basement? Twenty feet at most. If he just relaxed—or jumped to the top of the cage and clung to the fretwork?—he would not be hurt. He must not be hurt; the implications of the headlines would destroy him.

The elevator dived in darkness, far further than any conceivable excavation beneath the hotel. It fell through night, blacker and more terrifying than any moonless, starless reality. It plunged into total, unrelieved absence of light, a devastation to the senses, a mockery to the eyes.

Then, subtly, there was a difference. The blackness was still black but now it could be seen and valued. It was blackness, not blindness. Then increasingly there was a faint diminution of the darkness itself, and the shaft changed from sable to the deepest gray.

After they had fallen still further Lampley saw the shaft was lined with porcelain tiles, yellowed with neglect. Could it be they were no longer falling at all, just descending normally? To where?

They flashed past doors, cavernous rectangles in the shiny wall. Shiny? Yes, the tiles were brighter, cleaner, whiter. The cage slowed, came to a bouncing halt. The repressed fear surged through Lampley, making his feet and ankles weak and helpless. The clerk slid the door open smartly, with a sharp click.

"What's here?" asked the Governor, conscious of the inadequacy of the question.

"Odds," replied the clerk. "Odds. No ends to speak of but plenty of odds."

He half led, half pushed Lampley out of the elevator. They were in a great chamber, so far stretching that though it was adequately lit the defining walls were lost, far, far off. So close to each other that they almost touched, grand pianos with their lids thrown back and strings exposed, stood, rank after rank. From the ceiling long stalactites dripped on the pianos: plink plink, plink plink, plink plunk! A thousand piano-tuners might have been at work simultaneously.

"Nobody here," said the clerk. "All right." He turned swiftly back into the elevator, slamming the door.

"Wait!" cried Lampley in panic. "Wait for me." He heard the softly whirring mechanism as the elevator started, leaving him alone.

Lampley pounded the door with his fists. He shouted for the clerk to come back, not to desert him. He kicked the door. He screamed. Plink plink, plink plink, plink plunk.

He could die down here. He could die down here and no one would ever know it. He dared not go away from the elevator shaft—he might never find it again. He dared not stay—the clerk might not return until he was dead and the flesh rotted from his skeleton.

Plink plink. No, long before he died he would be raving mad. Plink plink. "Give us a tune at least," he pleaded. His voice produced no echo. No echo at all. Plink plunk.

Calm, almost ease, succeeded panic. He walked between the rows of pianos. They could not stretch to infinity, he reasoned, there must be an end to them somewhere. But reason also argued the pianos couldn't be here at all, there couldn't be seven or seventeen or seventy subbasements beneath the hotel. Once an impossibility happened there was no limit to the impossibilities to follow.

He had been six when Miss Brewster came to give him piano lessons. And is this our little Paderooski she asked so brightly. Do-do. C natural. Treble clef, base clef. Above the staff, below the staff. She smacked his hands when Mother wasn't looking. He kicked Miss Brewster's shins. After a while the lessons stopped.

A unicorn pranced out from between the pianos. His coat was white and sleek, his mane and tail shone like coal, his eyes were blue as sapphires. The long spiraling horn was pale gold, glistening bright. The Governor tried to approach him, to stroke the soft nose, to clutch the heavy mane. The unicorn stamped a nervous hoof and circled away, always barely out of reach. Lampley followed him down the long aisle between the pianos.

The unicorn looked back, his nostrils wide. Lampley put out his hand, almost touched him. The animal snorted, broke into a trot, a gallop. Its hooves pounded the hard floor: tata-rumpp, tata-rumpp, t-rump t-rump. The Governor ran too, shouting, calling. His lungs were sawed by jagged breaths, his heart burst through his ribs and left only a helpless, pounding pain behind. He wanted to stop, to give up, to faint; he kept on pursuing.

The unicorn paused, wary. He stamped a hoof, tossed his mane, pointed his horn. Lampley, gasping, was hardly able to totter forward. He took a step, two, leaned against the nearest piano. Plink, plink, plink, plink, plink plunk. The unicorn suddenly ran his horn into one of the instruments, withdrawing it to leave a splintered hole in the wood. A man came out of the shadows with a sledgehammer over his shoulder. He was a dwarf, naked to the waist, with writhing biceps, wearing a grease-matted brimless cap over thick curly hair. The growth on his chest curled also, an obscene felt. He swung the hammer down on the piano, smashing in the top, caving in one of the legs.

"What are you doing?" demanded Lampley before he realized he didn't care what the man was doing. "How do you get out of here?" he amended.

The dwarf went on methodically wrecking the piano. The unicorn disappeared, the sound of its hooves growing fainter and fainter. Lampley approached the dwarf, ready to clutch his shoulder, to extort a way out. He was afraid. Afraid of the blunt, lethal hammer, afraid of the strength and rage, which had reduced the piano to junk. Afraid of the answer to his question. Afraid there might be no answer.

The dwarf slung the maul back on his shoulder and walked away. The Governor wept. There was no strength in his arms or legs. He fell down and crawled weakly forward, sobbing and retching, the sour taste of vomit in his mouth. Plink plink, plink plink, plink plunk. Destruction of the offending piano made not the slightest difference in the cacophony.

The weight of all the floors above him, the overwhelmingly massive structure of steel and stone reaching to the surface, bowed him down in lonely, strangling terror. What mind, what mathematical faculty could estimate the thousands, the hundreds of thousands, the millions of crushing tons overhead, malign, implacable, waiting? He closed his eyes, moved his arms and legs convulsively. It was more than he could bear.

He was at the elevator again. If he could pry the door open perhaps he could climb the cables or brace himself between the rails on which the counterweights slid and inch his way upward. Or fall to destruction. He knew he could never get the door open. He was condemned to stay amid the pianos. He sobbed hopelessly.

Without belief he heard the sound of the machinery and the tip-tip-tip of the halting car. It was the young girl who opened the door and helped him in. She took a handkerchief, soft as fog, delicate as a petal, smelling of herself, and wiped his tears. She held his head between her breasts and he breathed in the scent of her untouched body. She pressed his wrists with her fingers. She put her hands under his arms and guided him against the wall of the cage.

"Thank you," he cried. "Oh thank you, thank you." He felt he was about to weep again, tears of shame and weakness. He held her tightly to reassure himself of the reality of the rescue, greedy for her gentle soothing. "Why did he do it? Tell me, why did he leave me down here?"

"Oh," she said, as though disappointed. "You want answers."

He shrank from her disapproval. "No, no. Please. I'm satisfied to be out of there."

She shut the door. The elevator shot upward, past the glistening white tiles, past the yellow ones, past the area of light. It rose—more slowly it seemed—through the darkness.

The creak of machinery increased, as though illumination were a lubricant and the deprived dark full of grit.

His heart was full of reverence and gratitude for her rescue, for her purity. He was bowed down by the simple fact of being alone with her in the cage. They passed the open grillwork of the first floor and ascended at snails' pace—no doubt now—to the second. She stopped the car, and taking his hand, led him out. He was thankful beyond counting when she took him to the bedroom, shutting the door behind them, and helped him out of his jacket. She wet a towel in the pitcher and bathed his face.

"You are very lovely," he said humbly. "As lovely as you are kind."

She took the paper cap from his head and smoothed his hair. If he had been humble, now he was humiliated beyond endurance. All that suffering, all that torture and anguish—with an absurd gaud perched atop him. It was beyond bearing. Fear and gratitude had not deprived him of all final dignity; the picture of the tissue paper cap jaunty upon him was too ridiculous for contemplation.

She smiled at him, magically healing his pride. Her mouth was a flower cut in soft pink stone. Her mouth was a velvet hope. Her mouth was red satin. She bent and touched him with it. He held his breath, felt himself tremble and die.

He kissed her, delicately, very delicately at first, savoring the soft, soft lips. He was dedicated to keeping her undefiled. He put his arms around her, touched his tongue-tip to her eyelids, her ears. He found her mouth again, pressed it tenderly. Then fiercely, lustfully, devouringly. She did not draw back. He lifted her shirt, intoxicating himself upon her small, perfect breasts.

"You will not hurt me?" she pleaded. "No man has been with me before."

He swore to himself he would not hurt her; it was not in him to be anything but loving. He would be wise, kind, compassionate; he would sacrifice his burning lust to her timidity. He would deflower her without rage.

He seized her, and seeing panic struggling against the consent in her eyes, ravished her brutally, violated her without thought of anything but his own triumph. Crying and reproaching himself, he begged her forgiveness. When she gave it, so readily, so understandingly, he repeated the act as heedlessly.

Remorse-stricken, he pressed his face against her knees, smoothed her long hair, kissed her temples, touched her body pleadingly. She smiled up at him, wound her arms around his so that their hands came together, palm to palm.

His penitence dissolved slowly in her grace. He remembered the creature downstairs—his son. "Are you her daughter?" he asked harshly.

She seemed to know whom he meant. "She is my sister."

"And the clerk?"

"The clerk?" She shook her head in incomprehension. She shut her eyes, breathing evenly.

Without disengaging himself from her he raised his head to look around. This was not his room. The furniture was similar, but the washstand was where the highboy had been, the highboy in the bureau's place. And the figures under the glass bell, the two dressed in black and white, were not the wedding couple but two duelists, crossing swords. Their faces were alike: father and son, older and younger brother, the same man at different periods. The older had got under the younger's guard and was pressing his advantage.

He should have phoned Mattie...no, Mattie was dead, the doctor shaking his enlightened head. The prognosis is always unfavorable unless we get it early...vulnerable womb... He should have phoned Marvin. It had been irresponsible of him to take this trip all by himself, impulsively, secretively, as though he were hiding something—he who could afford to have nothing to hide. And it had been doubly foolish to take this unusual, little-traveled route, to stop on whim at this obscure place.

He put his head down next to the girl's, feeling the comfort of her flesh against his body. He was not sleepy, no longer tired. She had refreshed and renewed him. He raised his head to look at her loveliness again.

The long hair was lusterless, streaked with gray. The smooth, fresh cheeks had relaxed into fatty lumps, coarse and raddled. The slack mouth turned downward, the flesh of her throat was loose and creepy. He pulled back in horror and saw that the tight, round breasts were long and flaccid, the flat belly soft and puffy, the slender arms and legs heavy and mottled.

Her eyes opened and looked dully into his. "What did you expect?" she asked.

He stood trembling by the side of the bed. "Only a little while ago…"

Her lips parted to show yellow teeth with gaps between. "There is no time here," she said and went back to sleep.

He did not look at her again, equally fearful of confirming or denying. Instead he picked up her clothes and scrutinized them as though they would reveal the truth. They were only the remembered white shirt and dark skirt, the small, narrow sandals, the flimsy scrap of underwear. By sight and scent they belonged to the girl who had brought him here, not to the woman on the bed.

He dressed with his back to her. The paper cap was on the floor where she had dropped it; he did not pick it up. He tiptoed out, avoiding noise, though the woman gave no sign of waking. He searched for his own room but none of the doors he opened showed the identifying arrangement of furniture or the wax figures of the wedding couple. He could not have confused the floor: he had climbed one flight from the lobby and the girl had taken the elevator only the same distance. If the elevator and the stairs were on different sides of the hotel...? That would account for the muddle.

The hall turned a corner. Instead of more doors it was blocked to its full width by a stairway. He took it in preference to retracing his steps; logically there would be a matching one back to the second floor further along.

Now the carpet under his feet was thick and soft instead of thin and sleazy. Strong bright light shone down from the floor above, showing walls paneled in pale wood, clean and elegant. It was a fleeting puzzle that this stairway should contrast so strongly—should have been preserved so carefully—with the rest of the hotel.

The sound of many voices, the clatter and movement of people came to him distantly. He reached the top. The third floor was decorated in pinks and grays: pink walls and ceiling, gray carpets, doors and woodwork. Couches and sofas occupied the wall-space not cut by doors. On the nearest one was sprawled an oversize rag doll onto which pendulous blue breasts had been carelessly sewn.

The hall was a large quadrangle with a square well in the center, guarded by a heavy wrought iron railing. The Governor rested his arms on the rail and gazed down at a concourse thronged with people. Women in sequined evening gowns, men in gaudy uniforms, gathered in knots, moved briskly, or sat idly on chairs and benches. A few of the women wore vivid strips of silk around their thighs or as skirts, the exposed parts of their bodies tattooed in blues and reds. A bearded man with shaggy hair had the skin of an animal caught over one shoulder. He saw a girl in hoopskirts, another in ruff and farthingale, but most wore the "formals" of his young manhood.

He had no feeling that this was a masquerade, a costume party: all wore their clothes with the assurance of habit, without self-consciousness of interest in the garb of others. Even at this distance he recognized a man in the green uniform of the United States Dragoons, obsolete since the 1840's, another in the white greatcoat of royal France. A Californio, silver pesoed trousers and all, talked earnestly with his companion in the dropped-waist sack of the Coolidge era while a hobble-skirted eavesdropper hovered close.

The throng was so tightly pressed together that Lampley did not at first make out the rococo fountain in the center. A sudden movement, a concerted parting, revealed its marble nymphs and cherubs spouting water in scatological attitudes. A sailor, wearing the characteristic British dickey, climbed to embrace one of the statues. He fell into the basin and was pulled out by an Attic shepherdess.

The Governor longed to join them, to dissolve his desires and disappointments in their gaiety and laughter. He knew there was no hope of happiness with them, as he knew there was no way for him to get down to them, but the knowledge did not quench his yearning.

He turned away and began circling the quadrangle. The doors on his right were all shut, no sound came from behind them. They were not consecutively numbered, nor in any conceivable order, not even in the same numerical system. 3103 was followed by 44, the next was XIX, then 900, 211, CCCV. One was marked with egg-shaped figures, which he took to be possibly Mayan. It was slightly ajar. He pushed it open.

It was a schoolroom. Disciplined desks marched side-by-side toward the teacher's raised podium hemmed in by blackboards gray with hastily erased chalk. Only the four seats in front were occupied. He tiptoed forward and slid into the second row. The teacher was a caricature Chinese mandarin with queue, emerald-buttoned skullcap, gold fingernail guards, tortoiseshell spectacles, brocaded robe.

"You have brought your homework?" he inquired, peering severely over the top of his spectacles.

"No sir," answered Lampley, getting up again.

"For what purpose does the honorable delegate arise?" mocked the teacher.

Lampley felt himself blushing. "I—I thought it was customary."

"All is custom as Herodotus said," remarked the teacher. "Herodotus was a barbarian," he explained genially to the class. "Sit down."

In front of Lampley sat a child with long blonde pigtails, one with a pink, the other with a white bow. She read aloud, "See little Almon. Little Almon lives with his mother and his uncle, Almon has the cat. Almon wants to play with the cat. The cat—"

"Quite enough," said the teacher. "Meditate."

The pupil next to the girl was the idiot. On the other side of the aisle were a boy of twelve and a girl a little older. When the girl turned her head Lampley saw her face was heavily bandaged. The Governor lifted the top of his desk and took out a book. It had no covers, the pages were torn and thumbed.

In the fifth year of the present reign, (he read) there appeared at court a magician from the East who claimed alcheminical learning to such a degree he was able to divine secret thoughts. A demonstration being required of him, he demanded that divers ladies-in-waiting who...

The Governor turned the page. The next leaf was written in runes. He riffled swiftly through the book. None of the rest of it was in the Latin alphabet. He turned back to the page he had read. The letters were all jumbled together, KJDRBWLSAYPZUQMXRQOTVBFLAIH, so that they made no sense. He held up his hand. The teacher pulled down his spectacles nearly to the end of his nose.

"No one is excused here," he announced. "Your attention, please."

Lampley let his hand fall. The children rustled and squirmed.

"I have here a button," said the teacher. "It is not a true button but a sort of courtesy button. It is in fact a mere plug, connected by the demon of electricity to an ingenious apparatus located in the antipodes of the Flowery, Middle or Celestial Kingdom. By pressing this button I can cause the instant and painless demise of an anonymous foreign devil. I repeat, the operation will cause the big-nosed one no distress at all; he will know nothing. By pushing the button I destroy him; also I bring untold happiness to all the sons of Han, whose rice bowls will then be full, whose fields, wives and concubines will be fertile, whose lords and tax gatherers will become unbelievably merciful. My problem: shall I press the button?"

He leaned back triumphantly in his chair and took from a desk drawer a bowl and chopsticks. Steam ascended from the bowl as the teacher deftly picked out long strings of noodles and sucked them into his mouth. Lampley could smell the sharp odor of the soup in the bowl. The class was silent while the teacher ate.

He put down the bowl and laid the chopsticks across it. "It is an ethical problem, you understand. Luckily, since I am unfitted for manual tasks—" he held up his fingernails for them to see—"I am absolved from considering it. I shall never have to press the button or not press the button."

Lampley raised his hand again.

"I told you no one is excused here," said the teacher.

"I was young," protested Lampley.

The teacher turned away disgustedly. He wrote on the blackboard in angular, unconnected letters, "Death knows no youth."

The pupils in the front row all turned around to stare at the Governor. The face of his son was set in a horrid grimace, teeth showing, eyes watering gummy white in the corners.

"She was ambitious for me. It seemed best at the time," muttered Lampley.

They all laughed together, snarling like dogs. Lampley hurled the book at them. The pages fluttered as it fell with a thud on the floor. The teacher wrote on the board in his singular script, Ambition, Doubt, Subservience, Conformity, Treachery, Heat, Bravery, Murder, Hope, Trifles, Treasure, Pity, Shame, Confession, Humility, Procreation, Final. "No alternatives!" he shouted.

CHAPTER THREE

THE Governor stumbled into the aisle and ran. Before the door a coffin rested on trestles. Tall candles burned at the head and foot. He did not have to look in to know it was Mattie or that beside her was the child she had never borne. He fell to his knees and crawled under the coffin. The trestles lowered; he had to squirm forward flat on his stomach to get clear of the casket. He got up and through the door, slamming it behind him.

The lights were bright as before but the people below had all disappeared. The fountain was dry; dust and lichen mottled the marble figures. Beneath the railing hung tattered battle-flags, dulled, tarnished, with great rips and tears. The floor, which he saw had been paved with great tile slabs, was broken and humped. Pale, sickly weeds thrust through the cracks. A sickening stench rose to make him gasp and turn away.

He had been seeking a stairway back to the second floor. He followed the quadrangle, came upon an unexpected hall between two rooms. At the end of the hall a square chamber was flooded with brilliance from a skylight. A legless man, many-chinned, frog-eyed, sat in a wheelchair. Across his monstrous chest a row of medals glittered. "Come in, come in," he roared jovially. "Any friend of nobody's a friend of mine."

"Can you tell me—" began the Governor.

"My boy," burst in the legless man, "if you want telling, I'm your pigeon; if I can't tell you no one can. I've shot cassowaries and peccaries, hunted dolphin and penguin, searched the seven seas for albatross and Charlie Ross. Oh the yarns I could spin about sin and tin and gin, about rounding the Horn in an August morn or lying becalmed in the horse latitudes with a cargo of bridles and harnesses. I've whaled off South Georgia, been jailed by Nova Zembla, failed on Easter Island, entailed in the West Indies. I'm a rip-roarer, a snip-snorter, a razzle-dazzle hearty-ho."

"You were a seaman?" asked the Governor politely.

"A seaman, v-d man, hard-a-lee man, a demon," sang the sailor. "Blast and damn me, I've fathered six hundred bastards in all colors—white don't count, naturally—from Chile to Chihili, from Timbuctoo to Kalamazoo. Have a drink."

The Governor looked around. On a long bar were ranged dozens of bottles, most of them empty. He picked up the nearest full one. It was cold, green, opened, and full of beer.

He put it to his lips, tilted it, realized his throat had been dry, parched. "Thanks," he muttered, taking it away reluctantly.

"Ah," said the cripple, "you should know the thanks I've had." He indicated his medals carelessly. "Decorated, cited, saluted, handshook, kissed on both cheeks. I've been thanked in Java and Ungava, in the Hebrides and the Celebes, in Tripoli and Trincomalee, in Lombok and Vladivostock. Have another drink."

"Thanks," repeated Lampley.

"Pleasure," responded the cripple. "Never drink alone, sleep alone, die alone. You haven't been here before?"

Lampley was puzzled how to answer. "Yes and no," he said at last.

The other nodded approvingly, tossed a ball into the air and caught it. "Caution. Many a poor sailor's been drowned dead because the captain or the mate yessed when he should have noed. Yes-and-no's a snug berth in a landlocked harbor."

"I only meant..."

The man had another ball in the air now. "The meaning of meaning. Semantics—that's a pun. Think you'll get the nomination?"

"It's touch and go," confessed the Governor. "I'm hoping."

The sailor was juggling three balls. He didn't look at them, just kept catching and tossing in rhythm. "Touch and go. Skill and chance," he said.

"That's right," agreed Lampley, drinking again.

"Comfortable?"

"Yes, thanks."

"Always said they should have put steam heat in here."

"But it's quite warm."

"Just wait till it snows. Drifts high as the roof, drifts high as the trees, drifts high as mountains. Buried in snow, white on top, green under the light here. A wonder we don't smother."

"Oh no," said the Governor, recalling the igloo in the refrigerator. "It's porous or something. The air comes through."

The juggler had seven balls and three oranges in the air. He added two empty bottles. "Nothing comes through. The outside never knows the inside, the inside's locked away from the outside."

"But it's always possible to break through," argued the Governor.

The juggler's arms were knotted muscles of skill. He had many bottles in the air besides the oranges and balls. "No man knows his fellow."

"Knowing and communicating are two different things."

"Yes and no," said the juggler judiciously. "You know a woman; do you…"

"Yes," insisted the Governor defiantly.

Still more bottles were tossed and caught. "You think so," said the juggler. "What happens when you fail?"

All the bottles were in play now. Deftly the juggler wriggled to the floor and added his wheelchair. "We fail yet nothing falls: the supremacy of perpetual motion. Try the fourth floor."

"There isn't any fourth floor," said Lampley.

"That's right. Try it."

Still juggling the balls, oranges, bottles and chair, the legless man threw himself into the air and joined the circle of whirling objects. The Governor left went through the passageway again to the quadrangle and looked over the railing. The fountain was gone. Goats nibbled at young trees growing through the obscured tiles. A man rode a pony listlessly and disappeared out of sight. A yellow wildcat prowled around, pausing to hiss menacingly at the goats. Lampley walked past closed doors, found himself in front of the elevator. He hadn't seen it—then it was there.

"Down," announced the clerk.

"I don't want…" began Lampley doubtfully.

"Going down," repeated the clerk firmly. "There's no up from here."

"How do all these people live?" asked the Governor. "The soldiers, the women, the school master, the juggler?"

The clerk shrugged. "No differently than anyone else. Osmosis. Symbiosis. Ventriloquism. Saprophytism. Necrophilism. The usual ways."

"Imagination? Illusion? Hallucination? Mirage?"

"We are what we are," said the clerk. "Can you say as much? Going down."

"I want to know," persisted Lampley.

"Don't we all? What's the use?"

The Governor temporized. "Will you let me off at my floor?"

"Do you know which it is?"

The Governor could not answer. He moved away from the elevator. There was a hole in the carpet going deep into the floor. In the hole was a heap of pennies, new-minted, bright coppery orange. He picked up a handful and sifted them through his fingers. None of them seemed to be dated, all had an eagle on one side and a scale on the other. A lump of untreated metal, hedgehog sharp, pricked his flesh. He dropped the pennies and put his hand to his mouth to suck the wound.

"Going down," the clerk called warningly.

Lampley said, "I only want—" The clerk slapped his knee, doubling with laughter. He did a little dance, his hands holding his abdomen. "Only!" he screamed between gusts of mirth. "Only! That's all. He only wants."

With what dignity he had left the Governor entered the elevator. The clerk, abruptly sober-faced, straightened up and shut the door. The openwork of the cage was now interwoven with rattan in which trailing fronds of greenery were stuck. Birds of somber hue—gray, black, slate, dark blue—climbed with silent intensity over the basketry, hung beak down from the roof, pecked quietly at the green. "Down."

Lampley held his breath, sucked in his stomach. But there was no sudden drop. The elevator glided with dignity past the second floor, the dim lobby without acceleration, into the dark depths. He strained his eyes for the first sign of light, of the tiled walls. Only the subtle sensations of descent told him they were not stopped, rigid, just below the first floor.

The clerk said, "The teacher has a list of all those who cheated."

"It must be long."

"It's not as long as the guilty think, nor as short as the innocent believe."

"A youthful indiscretion," said the Governor lightly.

"The piano-smasher knows all about false references."

"Everyone does it," said the Governor. "You have to, to get a job."

"The juggler has suffered from the effects of kicked-back commissions."

"The custom is old. Who was I to change it?"

"The people in the concourse voted to send a man to the legislature who promised to do certain things."

"Campaign oratory," said the Governor.

"The girl—"

"Stop," ordered the Governor. "Are you taking it on yourself to punish sins?"

"Ah," said the clerk. "You think absolution should be automatic, instant and painless?"

Lampley thought, if I had a heavy wrench or a knife or a gun I could kill him and no one would know. His fingers tingled, his knees ached. He tried to speak casually, to stop any further words the clerk might utter. As he sought for some innocuous topic he saw the walls lighten, recognized the yellowed tiles.

The clerk bent over the control lever as though in prayer, the birds were all still and unmoving. Passing the shining white tiles Lampley strained to catch the faint sound of the pianos. He could not be sure he heard it, still less that he hadn't. The walls of the shaft gradually became a pale green, deepening into sky-blue so natural they seemed to expand outward.

Smoothly the elevator tilted at an angle just steep enough to force him to put one foot on the side of the cage in order to stay upright. The clerk, clinging to the lever, had no trouble. They slid down the incline at moderate speed. The tiled walls fell away; they were traveling on a sort of funicular diagonally through the floors of a vast department store. Counters of chinaware were set parallel and perpendicular, the cups and dishes cunningly tilted to catch the light: experimental, modern, conventional, traditional, all the familiar patterns including sets and sets of blue willow ware. Some of the pieces were so curiously shaped it was impossible to guess their use: platters with humps in their centers, cups pierced with holes, plates shaped like partly open bivalves, cones, spheres and pyramids with handles but no apparent openings.

They passed a millinery department where women were trying on feathered helmets, fur busbies, brass-and-leather shakos, woolen balaclavas, wide-brimmed straws, tight-fitting caps of interwoven fresh flowers. Lampley saw they were all using long hatpins, jamming them recklessly through the headgear under consideration. The discarded hats were not put back in stock but thrown into large wastebaskets.

The spaces between floors were open, revealing the heavy steel girders with which they were braced. Through the openings in the girders lean dogs chased scurrying rats, snakes twined themselves, bats hung upside-down, land-crabs scuttled, stopping only to turn their eye-stalks balefully toward the elevator.

On another floor lined with mirrors that shot their dazzle into his eyes like a volley of arrows, more women pulled and tugged girdles over obstinate hips with concentrated effort, bending reverently over unfolded brassieres to match the arbitrary cups against overflowing breasts, holding up corsets, which coldly mocked. Breech-clouted boys waved huge fans, stirring the piles of garments on the tables.

The elevator continued downward. Shoppers strolled by book counters with untempted glances, heading for the infants' wear to examine tiny shirts, diapers, kimonos, blankets, fingering the embroidery, pursing lips, smiling, shaking their heads. They stood abstractedly before bright prints, sat stiffly on padded chairs, thumped mattresses, fiddled with gifts and notions.

On a lower floor overhead lights glared down on roulette tables, card games where the players squinted suspiciously ever their hands, blankets on which dice-throwers were shooting craps. The walls were covered with posters: LAMPLEY FOR SUPERVISOR; A VOTE FOR LAMPLEY IS A VOTE FOR YOU! The Governor was puzzled; he had never run for that office.

The walls closed in again, the elevator tilted further, so that the Governor was sitting on the side of the cage. It picked up speed now, whizzing along, rounding banked curves, allowing momentary glimpses of open spaces like railroad stations. "How far are you going?" Lampley asked.

"Not far," said the clerk, coming out of his lethargy, "We're almost there."

"Where?"

"There. Where else?"

They rounded another curve and shot down a grade. A bird near the Governor ruffled its feathers sleepily. "I just want to get back."

"Who doesn't?" demanded the clerk harshly.

The walls of the shaft—it was a tunnel now—were transparent. There was water pressing against them, a powerful stream judging by the exertions of the fish swimming against it. They ran a long way through the river—Lampley was sure it was a river from occasional sight of a far-off, muddy bank—and there the glass walls showed only earth, with the roots of trees reaching down and piling up baffled, against them.

The walls became opaque, then vanished. They were running down the side of a mountain covered with patches of snow. In places the snow was piled in great drifts, carved by winds into tortured peaks; elsewhere it lay in thin ruffled streaks and ovals. Out of these shallow patches dark bushes sprang bearing red and yellow fruit. The bare spaces between the snow were of moist, eroded, earth where small brown plants grew spikil.

The Governor could not see the sky nor the roof of the cavern—if they were in some sort of cavern—only the ridges and spurs of the mountain slope. There were scars on the rugged ground as from landslides, great bites where the drop was sheer and jagged rocks stood out like drifting teeth, but none of the slips could have been recent for the mounds at their feet were firm-looking and grassy. They rounded still another curve and the elevator slowed to a stop.

The clerk, who had clung protectively to the controls, straightened up and looked inquiringly over his shoulder. Lampley stared back at him. "All out," said the clerk, waving his hands. The birds fluttered, cawed and shrieked, flying through the open door with an angry whir of wings. They wheeled in uncertain circles and then made off in small, separate flights. "All out," he repeated.

"I don't want to get out," said Lampley. "There's nothing for me here."

"Are you sure?" asked the clerk.

"I…" Lampley paused, uncertain.

"You see?" demanded the clerk triumphantly.

Resigned, the Governor made his way out. The clerk smiled at him, not unfriendly, and Lampley almost begged him not to leave, not to abandon him but to take him back. If the right words came to his tongue, if the earnest feeling projected them into sound, he was sure he would not be deserted. Then the elevator started slowly backing, gathering speed as it went, running silently, shrinking in size until it was merely a small speck on the side of the slope. Only the terminal bumpers and the greasy track on which it had run remained.

CHAPTER FOUR

LAMPLEY looked about him. Mountains shut off every horizon; the near ones sharp, serrated, detailed, those far-off hazy, soft and rounded. It was impossible to make out the character of the more remote, but those on either side gradually melted into foothills with twisting streams appearing from between shoulders and disappearing again behind ridges. The light overhead, nebulous, indefinite, emanated from no discernible body. It had the quality of sunlight filtered through thin clouds, soothing to the eye as the balmy air was pleasant to the skin. He felt refreshed.

Beneath his feet a fan-shaped plateau canted downward until it merged with a mighty plain far off, a plain enclosing a vast lake. A broad river meandered across the plateau and continued, as near as he could tell, on the plain below. Dense blue-green grass grew lushly, heavily powdered with yellow, white, and purple violets, dandelions, daisies, buttercups and tiny pale blue flowers. The Governor took off his shoes and socks, stuffing the socks into the shoes and knotting the laces together. He slung them over his shoulder. The grass felt electric, rejuvenating his feet as he trod on it.

A black fox crossed his path and paused to stare over his sharp nose before continuing on. A squirrel balanced its body erect for a swift, curious scrutiny before it was off with a flick of its tail. Other small animals bounded past him, none seemed afraid. He thought he saw deer in the distance, and a bear, but he was not sure.

He came to a bank of the river and followed it down. He could see now it was joined by a number of tributaries before it emptied into the blue, unruffled lake. Other rivers foamed down the more rugged mountains on each side of the plain, all made their way to the lake, which seemed to have an island in it, a long way from shore.

When he reached a confluence with one of the branches he hesitated and followed the smaller stream back until he came to a place where it was crossed by high, flat-topped steppingstones nosed into the splashing and spuming water. He tested the rocks gingerly, but they were firm, and though wet, not slippery. Each time his progress was stopped by such a meeting he found a similar set of stones not far away.

Nearing the lake he saw its color was a warm blue, with violet tones. There was no hint of paleness in it; it was majestic, assured, unique. He quickened his pace. The island assumed more definite shape. It was large and irregular, with capes and promontories thrusting out into the lake. Heavily wooded, willows came down to the shore, behind them oaks and maples spread red and yellow leaves. Still further back the blue tips of firs pointed above.

He came to the shore, a rocky beach, where the water lay perfectly still over and between round, mossy stones. He waded in; the water was delightfully cool without a suggestion of coldness. He reached down and laved his face with it. When he straightened up he saw a rowboat a little further out, unanchored, its bow resting on the rocks, its stern hardly moving. The boat was the color of the lake save for a silvery trim and silvery oars were neatly shipped in bright metal rowlocks.

The Governor made his way carefully to the boat, freeing it from the rocks. He climbed in, laid his shoes in the stern, began rowing toward the island. After a few strokes he paused and looked upward. The haze was evidently permanent, which might somehow account for the unvarying, equable climate. He shipped the oars and allowed the boat to drift. A fish jumped in the water and splashed a widening circle. A bird, white and gold with carmine beak, flew overhead. Everything was serene.

There was no wind but there seemed to be a weak current, for the boat drifted very slowly, equidistant between the shore and the island. The features he had noticed before became more differentiated; he noted a number of land spits, small coves, moon shaped beaches. The woods did not everywhere come right down to the water; in places they retreated to make room for soft green meadows. He picked up the oars and rowed a long distance before coming even with a particularly inviting cove.

He debated whether or not there might be a still more desirable one farther along. The temptation to refuse decision was great. It was with a distinct effort that he turned the bow and ran the boat ashore.

The sands were fine and soft and golden, darkening a short way from the lake into a pale brown border between the beach and the greensward. He stepped out of the boat and hauled it clear of the water. Impulsively he took off his clothes and put them with his shoes. He rolled on the grass like a boy on a horse. The grass was soft as down, yet springy and lithe beneath his body. He lay prone, snuffing in the smell of the bruised stems. He stretched out his hands to reach into a patch of clover with the idle thought that one of them might be four-leafed. He saw with horror he was reaching with the reddish, vestigial, unteachable hands on foreshortened arms of his son.

He felt sweat on his forehead as he shivered in terror. He jumped up and ran for the boat, slipping and sliding on the crushed grass. He lay trembling, eyes shut. Fearfully he drew his hands toward him and opened his eyes. These were his own hands, familiar, middle-aged and freckled, normally colored, still fairly smooth despite the raised veins, still cunning to hold and twist and manipulate. His own hands, attached to his own arms. Shaken, he sighed in shuddering relief.

He walked slowly over the grass toward the interior of the island. Under the nearest trees—larch, beech, hickory—wild strawberries grew thickly. He picked quantities of the elusive fruit, crushing it with his tongue against the roof of his mouth, enjoying its sweetness, allowing the juice to trickle slowly, deliciously down his throat. He had not tasted wild strawberries since the day he and Mattie decided to get married (No children till we can give them the things they should have).

The trees were well spaced, letting the light enter freely between them. There was no young growth, no saplings; all the trees were full grown and healthy, with no sign of deadfalls or rotted logs. Only, far apart, raspberry canes bearing their garnet, black, white or green thimbles.

The trees didn't thin, they stopped abruptly. Ahead was a natural clearing; in the center of the clearing a jungle growth of stalks and vines rose in a high and inextricably tangled mound. Lampley advanced, irresistibly attracted. He tried to part the interwoven stems but they refused to give. On the ground were flat stones, some with sharp edges. He picked up a fair-sized one and went back to the woods. With some trouble he used it to saw off an oak branch.

He shaped the club to the right heft and bound the stone to it with vines. He was dubious of its strength and his doubts proved justified when, after hacking through some of the growth, the head came loose. With new patience he reaffixed it and continued to cut away. His arms began to ache; short, blinding flashes darted behind his eyes. He persisted; there was no reason, no goal—he was simply impelled to clear his way into whatever lay hidden by the tangle.

After refitting his crude ax again and again, he tore away the loosened vines to reveal a white stone column, tapered slightly at base and capital, its smooth sides spotted with the marks of the sucking disks and clinging tendrils he had torn free. Beyond the column he was faced by an enclosed, roofed rectangle. In this dim area no vines grew except the sickly, inhibited, baffled ends whose invading thrust had faltered in complete discouragement. Doubling back, they had interwoven in their attempt to return to the light, but they had not been able to make a curtain impervious enough to prevent him seeing the backs of the other pillars and the high roof they supported.

He shouldered his way in and peered through the dusk to make out a table flanked by two wide couches. Both table and couches were of the same stone as the columns—marble, Lampley guessed—the couches piled with soft furs. He took a tentative step forward.

Something glinted dully on the table; it was a bronze ax. He picked it up, balanced it, tried the edge with his thumb. It was reasonably sharp and the handle was firmly fitted into the head.

With mounting enthusiasm he attacked the vines from the rear, chopping and slicing, confident in this fine tool. Triumphantly he cleared the space between two pillars, dragged the cut growth clear; returned to his task. He freed another pillar, opened another space, dragged more vines away.

Now the interior was lucid enough to show the floor as one large mosaic of gleaming stones. The picture they composed was of a central fire, the flames red, blue and yellow, surrounded by smaller, less brilliant fires. On the outer edge animals turned their heads toward the warmth: horses, oxen, elephants, lynx, hippopotami, wolves, lions, zebras, elk.

He resumed his work, finished clearing one of the long sides and pulling down the severed branches from the roof before stopping again. Backing away to the trees he saw the building was so simple in design, so artfully proportioned, that it might have grown in this spot. The low pitched roof was copper, untarnished, like the new-minted pennies he had picked up in the hotel.

There was almost full visibility inside the little temple now; on impulse he hacked holes in the ivy on the other three sides for crude windows. The fresh light illuminated the ceiling, intricately painted in abstract designs with colors as bright as those of the mosaic. The table and couches were the only furniture, but on the floor, neatly laid out against columns, was a variety of fishing equipment.

He picked up a rod and held it out. It was limber, fitted with silk line and a dry fly. A searching vine-tip had tried to loop around the reel; he disentangled it. Carrying the rod, he left the temple and sauntered into the woods. There were no paths, no need of any beneath the widely spaced trees, yet he seemed to be following a definite avenue, broad and almost straight. Despite his nakedness and recent exertions he felt no chill in the shade; there was no tiredness in his muscles nor discomfort from the ground under his feet.

He passed natural clearings where saplings had not encroached upon the low-growing plants he recognized as edible, though clearly uncultivated. There were peas and beans of strange species, large and succulent, spattered with rainbow tints, purple melons, green cucumbers, golden-yellow leeks and onions as well as unfamiliar shrubs with broad green leaves and many kinds of flowers.

In a much larger clearing there was a pool of the same deep blue as the lake, roughly oval and perhaps twice the size of the little temple. At one end rushes grew tall, at the other, lotus offered their heavy flowers haughtily upward. The rest of the pool was covered with waterlilies and lilypads on which there was constant movement.

He thought they must be teeming with water-beetles or very small frogs; when he squatted at the water's edge he discovered the figures to be tiny men and women leaping and frolicking on the moss, rolling smooth pebbles tall as themselves, swimming out to the pads, climbing the lilies and diving from them, sporting in the water, showing no signs of alarm at his presence.

He lay down flat for a closer look. Some wore loincloths or loose robes, most did not. Their graceful movements accented their strength and endurance; they performed feats easily, which, if done in proportion by any full-sized man would have exhausted him quickly, yet these went from one game to another without flagging. They moved so swiftly it was hard to estimate their number; he thought there might be fifty of them here. He had no way of knowing if this was all of them or whether those in sight constituted a part of their number, with the rest engaged, perhaps, in less active pursuits.

As he became accustomed enough to tell them apart he saw there were no children among them. Lampley could understand why they should segregate their young, for some of their amusements were startling even to a worldly adult; however the simpler variations suggested that they did perpetuate themselves in the customary way. Except when forced by circumstance to take a position on obscene literature, sex-offences or unconventional behavior, Lampley was morally relaxed; he viewed their recreation with the detached interest of an anthropologist, the appreciation of an aesthete, the envy of a man past his youth. He remained silent and watched for quite some time.

He noticed one female wandering apart from the rest, neither joining the others—nor being sought by them. He thought there was dejection or despondency in the set of her shoulders, in the aimless way she placed one slender leg before the other or clasped her hands behind her neck. All of the tiny people were exquisite, but she, because of her repose and aloofness, seemed even more beautiful than the others.

Without quite intending to, he reached out his free hand and lifted her close to his face.

She gave no sign of surprise or fear, but stared back into his eyes whose irises were the size of her head. He marveled at the fineness of her features, the flowing lines of her body, the gracefulness of her arms and legs, the regal carriage of her head. Her loveliness was poignant and perfect. He could not take his eyes from her.

It was impossible for him to put her down again, to part from her, to walk away as though he had not touched and held her. Guiltily, furtively, he carried her back to the temple, holding her against his chest, fearful that the beating of his heart must be a frightening thunder in her ears. He told himself he would not keep her long; before she was missed he would take her back.

He placed her on the table and sat on the couch admiring her. The diminutive face was haughty and sullen but in no way distressed. Her dark hair was piled on top of her head, falling with seeming artlessness to her shoulders, her breasts were high and taut-round, defiant shields—her thighs long and sleek. Even allowing for the difficulty of discerning blemish in so small a being, the glowing color, pale yet warm, the smooth hands and feet, the clustered body hair, all spoke of such flawlessness that he had to control his fingers lest they close in upon her to squeeze out the essence of beauty.

He whispered, "Do you hear me? Can you understand me?"

She moved her head slightly aside. Whether from outrage, annoyance or indifference he could not tell. He did not think it was incomprehension. When he repeated his questions she made no response at all.

She seemed to weary; he thought he detected an effort to keep her head erect, her eyelids from drooping. He placed her gently on the couch, ran a fingertip lightly over her side.

She trembled and stiffened. When he took his hand away she curled in a graceful pose and closed her eyes. He covered her with one of the furs from the other couch; she did not move.

He picked up the fishing rod from where he dropped it outside when he had brought her in. The vines appeared to have grown; he must chop them closer, root them out if possible, clear the remaining sides entirely. There was no reason to allow the temple to be covered again.

He strode purposefully back to the lake. By chance he did not arrive at the cove where the boat was but further along the shore where a narrow pier, no more than a series of poles stuck into the lake bottom with planks laid on the cross-pieces, jutted out a few yards over the water.

He walked to the end and gazed into the clear depths. Marine flowers—vegetable, mineral or animal—wavered in a multitude of bright hues. Swimming, basking, or feeding among them were myriads of translucent fish, large and small, silver, blue, red, orange, green, nacreous gray. Below them flatfish moved slowly, rippling their bodies in lazy humps. Above them torpedo-shaped swimmers sped madly with barely perceptible flicks of tail and fins. Just under the surface, breaking into the air every now and then, thickly clustered schools of shiny fingerlings raced and darted in confusion.

Lampley was not a practiced angler, he was dubious of his ability to cast the dry fly and he saw he had brought along the wrong equipment. He let out a length of line awkwardly and watched the fly float on the surface, then very slowly sink downward. The excitement, which had fevered him since he came upon the figures at the pool, subsided. He was content.

The crimson fish shot from nowhere at the now invisible fly and the rod jumped almost from his hands as the reel unwound. The fish ran out toward the channel, the line lifting clear, like a knife cutting up through jelly. It circled and leapt, a dazzling blot of whirling color against the lake's placid blue.

He gained back considerable line before the fish ran again. He reeled in, the fish dived; each time it took less line. At last Lampley brought it gasping and thrashing on its side to the end of the pier. Lying flat, he was able to reach down and hook two fingers under the distending gills to lift it into the air.

He carried the fish back to the temple. The vines were winding around the base of the columns again; loose tendrils crept toward each other, ready to intertwine upon meeting. He came in nervously, eyes averted, as though by deliberately not searching for her he would assure her still being there. She was on the couch where he had left her, one tiny arm— was his memory playing him tricks? It did not seem so small as it had—thrown over her eyes.

He had no knife to scale the fish, no fire to cook it. He was not hungry himself but his captive might be. He put his rod away, took the bronze ax and the fish outside. With the edge of the ax he managed clumsily to cut the flesh from the backbone in a crude filet, then he scraped the filet free of the skin. Tentatively he tasted a piece; it was delicious.

He wished for a gold platter on which to serve food to her. He longed for a retinue of slaves to prepare her meal, an army of servants to wait on her. He stood by the couch, sadly deficient, a slice of raw fish in either hand, eager, tremulous, yet happy.

The woman stirred, opened her eyes, threw off the fur cover with some effort. She stood erect, stretching, shuddering in obvious pleasure, pointing first one leg and then the other, massaging her flanks and stomach sensuously. She had unquestionably grown larger: he could see the faint, fine down on her arms now, the intricate convolutions of her ears, the roundness of her navel. She was the length of his hand instead of less than that of his finger.

He made his voice as low as he could. "Would you like to eat?"

She turned to him as though she had not been aware of his presence until he spoke, but having learned of it was completely unaffected. She stretched again and looked up at him disdainfully. With some difficulty he broke off a crumb of the fish and offered it to her. Her glance did not waver from his face; she reached out her hands and accepted the morsel, nibbling it daintily, still staring at him. When she had eaten it he offered more; she turned away and re-settled herself on the fur, her back to him, her hip curving high.

He put the rest of the fish on the table and took up the ax. He trimmed the new growth of vine down to the ground and cleared one of the short sides. He stopped to sharpen the ax on the stone he had used for cutting before he discovered it. He freed a corner pillar on the opposite long side before he put up the ax and went to the pool.

It was deserted. Had he caused them to leave, or brought some worse disaster on them by stealing the woman! He ran his fingers through the moss, peered intently at the water plants—they were gone. He was not cruel or unreasonable; if she would only communicate with him he would do anything she asked.

He twisted a flat leaf into a cone-shaped cup and filled it with water. It leaked only one slow drop at a time, a growing, fat, wet pearl, which swelled until its weight detached it. Lampley felt quite complacent over his cleverness in contriving so tight a cup. He returned to the temple and sat on the other couch, watching her sleep, holding the water in readiness. She had not covered herself; she was now the length of his forearm.

He must have been too intent. She moved and turned, opened her eyes and stared back at him indignantly. She did not make the slightest attempt to hide any part of her body from him; she seemed to taunt him with its promise, so impossible of fulfillment. His hand shook as he held the leaf out to her. She grasped it and drank, smiling secretively. Instead of returning it she threw it on the floor, spilling out the water that was left.

"Would you like to go back to the pool?" he asked.

She did not answer; her full-lipped mouth set in a cruel line. It had been a stupid question; she was tall enough to slide off the couch without help and walk to the pool. Tears came to his eyes and his throat ached at the thought of no longer being able to hold her in his hand. He implored her to forgive him for having carried her away, he pled with her to speak to him. He put his ear close to her mouth to hear her words if she spoke.

She allowed the set of her lips to change without softening. She moved to the opposite end of the couch, tidying her hair, twisting her head as though looking in a mirror. He reached out, hesitated, touched her. He ran his hands and lips over her body, fondled her, half in abject pleading, half in equally abject desire. She trembled; he knew it was with rage and loathing, not fear.

With the ax he fell upon the remaining vines, cut them to the earth. Those he had mutilated before were growing again but they were not high enough to give him release in chopping them down. When the temple was cleared all around he came in again and stood looking at her. She was still taller, still unrelenting. If he had originally wooed instead of capturing her she could not have regarded him so.

Remorseful, he went once again to the pool. The lotus blossoms had gone, leaving the dry pods swaying stiffly. The rushes and water lilies were brown and brittle, the moss was fuzzy in decay, the edges of the lilypads were softly rotting. The small people had returned, unchanged in size—she alone had grown, afflicted by the wrong he had done. They lay near the edge of the pool in listless attitudes. Their hair had turned gray or white, they had lost their suppleness, paunches and wrinkles were visible.

He went away from them, walking slowly through the woods, glancing up at the light or down at the soft humus underfoot. The trees stopped short before a saucer-like meadow. Milky-blue poppies grew so thickly their petals crushed against each other, hiding the stems and ground beneath. He plunged into them, then halted; sharp stones hurt his feet.

He bent down and pushed the flowers apart. Their roots grew in twinkling, winking emeralds and rubies of all sizes and cuts. They were packed loosely enough for air and water to seep in, tightly enough to make it not easy to work them free and gather a handful. He tried to select the largest stones, discarding one for another, moving deeper into the field. His hands and cradled arms full, he let them drop and chose the smaller, more evenly matched gems. He threw all these away also and began all over; whatever combinations of size, cut or color he picked up did not equal the possibilities of this profusion.

Dissatisfied, he turned from the poppies. They had called to him, promising, then promised again and yet again. He could not—with a handful of stones such as these—say the promise had not been kept; he could not say it had.

He paused to bathe his bruised feet in the pool. The lotus plants had disappeared completely, the rushes drooped brokenly, the lilies floated like scraps of worthless paper, the lilypads were limp and soggy. The little people had lost their hair and much of their flesh, their skins stretched over protruding bones. They did not move save to turn over a weary hand or draw up a cramped leg.

He came to the temple. The persistent vines had again begun their climb up the pillars. The woman stood on the couch, her hands over her breasts, fingers open around the nipples. Her head was level with his chest; she tilted it to look at him with the same inexorable hate. He poured the rubies and emeralds at her feet. She glanced down, kicked a fur casually over them.

"I thought you might like them," he mumbled. "They...they..."

She hunched up one shoulder. He was sure she understood his words.

"Are you hungry?" he asked, then he saw she had eaten more of the fish. "Are you thirsty?"

She threw herself down on the furs, buried her face in her elbow. Resentfully he took the ax and cut back the vines. Those he had chopped down at first were dry and brittle; they would burn if he had some way of making fire. He gathered a trailing handful and brought them inside. Her back was turned as he arranged them on the mosaic. He laid the flat stone next to them and struck it slantwise with the ax. Some of the blows resulted in futile sparks but the stems did not ignite.

He gave up; with the fishing rod he returned to the lake. He pushed the boat into the water and rowed with the current past the pier, heading for the deeper parts. He laid the rod over the stern and let the way of the boat pull the line slowly from the reel. The fly stayed on the surface.

His eyes searched the further shore. Some of the distant mountain peaks were bare, others were forested to the top. Some fell in palisaded steps down to the plain, some descended in series of rounded hills, some sloped evenly.

Nearly all carried rivers to the lake. There were no signs of any way out of the cavern.

On the island side, great trees grew out over the water. From their boughs fell seedpods, which floated diagonally across the current to the other shore. Waiting for them at the edge of an extensive swamp were yellow swans with black beaks that stretched their long necks to gobble the prizes. They fought among themselves for the tidbits, flapping their wings, rising partway into the air, twisting, their webbed feet tightly curled.

Past the overhanging trees the island curved inward in a wide, crescent-shaped beach of blue sand. He was tempted to land but the current carried him on before he could make up his mind. He passed a flat cape and low bluffs against which the calm lake churned white. He thought he made out the ruins of a castle far behind the bluffs, but the quality of the light changed from soft to hazy; what appeared to be ruins might as well be a natural formation of rock.

He guessed he must be halfway around the island; it was easier to drift on than row against the current. On the opposite shore animals had come down to drink, tapirs and zebus, raccoons and gazelles, llamas and koala bears. A few raised their heads as he passed, the majority paid no attention.

There was a ruffling of the water and an ominous sucking sound as the tide changed its easy momentum into an irresistible pull. Furiously the boat was whirled around—stern, bow, bow, stern—in a dizzying circle. He rowed with all his might, feathering his oars in panic as often as not, almost falling backward as they failed to bite. He half rose, digging them in, pulling desperately, returning, pulling with all his strength. The boat steadied; the bow pointed straight ahead. Almost as quickly as he had been caught in the vortex he was free of it. He inhaled raspingly, dropping his head on his chest.

The lake widened; it was so far across he could barely make out details on the mainland. The island changed character; forbidding basalt walled it, interrupted by inlets where the water surged in sullen, angry obstinacy. Foam gushed and spouted from great holes in the rocks, adding to the tumult. Lampley thought he saw ships in one of the inlets—high-prowed, single-masted vessels with low freeboards guarded by overlapping shields—but like the ruined castle they could have been oddly shaped masses of rock.

He must have almost circled the island, for he saw the plain he had followed from the elevator on the further shore. This part of the lake was placid and the undertow negligible. He put up his oars and took the rod in his hands, pulling at it so the fly skipped lightly over the water.

The fish was green and gold, pure colors, unsullied. It was clearly too heavy for the line. Lampley played it—awkwardly—exhausted it, brought it to the boat and unhooked it to lie, flopping and dying and turning a mottled brown, on the floorboards. He looked down at the cruel, voracious mouth and felt his own setting in similar lines. He rowed to the island and landed on an unsheltered beach of reddish sand.

It was a long way to the temple; he began to think he had missed it when he saw the roof and columns ahead. The vines had made great progress in his absence; in places they had reached the eaves and were writhing over the cornice.

She was leaning against a pillar, facing him, one hip slouched lower than the other. She was nearly four feet tall; her proportions had not altered, nor did her increased size reveal any imperfection. He was shaken by the same mixture of awe and lust, admiration and avidity.

When he showed her the fish she went to the table and taking the scrap left of the first one, threw it out. The emeralds and rubies lay disregarded on the furs, the pile of withered vines was as he had left it. He waited with diminishing hope for her to give some further recognition of his presence. "I have been all around the island," he said, knowing she would not acknowledge his speech.

He cleared the vines away, wondering if she approved his industry. He explored the woods until he found a plant on which gourds had dried. He kicked one, broke off the neck, filled it at the pool. There were no signs of her people. The gourd did not leak at all as he carried it back.

She had divided the fish in half, skinned and boned it less wastefully than he had the other. She was able to work at the table now, though with some difficulty. Tall as a very small woman she yet retained the tantalizing, provocative, shameful appeal of her original size. He set the gourd down shakily.

She took it up as though it had been there all along and she had only now come to need it, and poured half its contents over herself. It seemed to him, weak with longing, that she displayed an added, lazy insolence as she smoothed the water over her breasts and under her arms, moving in studied tempo, reveling in the pleasure of her own touch. She walked slowly to the vines and dried herself carefully, over and over. She neither concealed nor displayed her body; she acted as though she were alone.

He put his hand on her arm, she looked up at him in the simulated surprise of cold inquiry. Her lips were pressed together, but not so firmly as to disfigure their symmetry. Her eyes were gray, with green and golden flecks; the slight droop of the lids emphasized her look of disdain. Her skin was smooth as glass. He could wait no longer. He was consumed with desire for her.

He clasped her, lifted her, threw her on the couch, began kissing her gluttonously. He tried, first with cunning, then with violence, to part her lips, to move her arms from their rigid position. She remained completely passive, her eyes wide open in their implacable scorn. He paused in his onslaught, begged her to forgive him, to say something, to voice even a rejection. She lay silent, unmoving, unresisting as he wept and shouted.

His hands dug into her shoulders, caressed, gripped, pulled at her body. His mouth smothered hers. He closed his eyes to shut out her derision, opened them again to see if she had relented. He pressed himself against her, forced his body into hers. The shock telegraphed back to him.

She became wild and wanton and responsive. She was avid, insatiable, shameless. She exhausted him, drained him, wore him into incapacity, then invited, teased, coaxed, compelled him into fresh lechery. The element of the perverse, inherent in her size, her captivity, her unveiled loathing, added the final touch to their ecstasy. They came together again and again without concession in a rape of the courtesan, wringing joy out of their enmity.

When he collapsed, exhausted but less than content, she calmly rose and drank thirstily from the gourd. He watched her easy, fluent movements, knowing she was conscious of him and of their embrace, knowing that it signified no intimacy to her, that she was untouched. "Won't you forgive me?" he begged. "Won't you speak, or at least show you hear?"

She combed her long hair with her fingers and twisted it deftly into place. She lifted one leg, bent at the knee, and studied her foot. She sauntered to the columns and stood at the edge of the temple looking out, her back to him.

He made himself get up and go to her, kneeling at her feet. Even in his abjection he could not refrain from embracing her legs, resting his cheek against her flesh. She stood quietly, as though waiting for his next move. When he did nothing beyond implore her pardon, she disengaged herself calmly, turned away, and walked to the opposite row of columns.

It no longer seemed imperative to keep the vines chopped down. He let them grow at will except on the one side he kept cleared. Though he knew no hunger save for her, he fished and fetched water for her to drink and bathe. He thought she must tire of the monotonous diet, remembering the berries he brought her gourdsful. She ate them greedily. When her mouth was stained with the juice he could not control his longing; he took her once more. She responded as before; as before she remained inviolable.

She grew no more, and this pleased him, guaranteeing as it did a continued mutual enslavement. In mid-cycle between his despair after forcing her and helplessness before doing so again, he gloated over her smallness, her estrangement from everyone but him.

He did not return to the pool. Instead, he made the longer journey to the lake for water. He went back to the poppies by a roundabout route, picked an armful, leaving the gems in which they were rooted undisturbed. She let them lie at her feet where he had placed them.

On his next homecoming to the temple she had made a fire, succeeding where he had failed. It burned swiftly on the mosaic, consuming the dried vines as quickly as she could feed them to it. He took the ax and cut some green boughs, chopping them into convenient lengths. With these and the vines the fire could be kept alive, smoking, not giving out any warmth, but adequate to cook the fish he caught.

She took a portion of whatever he brought her—fish, fruit, flowers—and sacrificed it in the fire. When she was not sleeping, bathing, preening or standing looking out, she sat beside the embers, quiet, absorbed. Though he knew her indifference was unfeigned, this additional withdrawal added to his torment. When it became unendurable—when his lust and pique and desire to master her overcame his submissiveness—he attacked her and met her raging passion.

Otherwise she did not acknowledge his presence directly. She put his portion of cooked food on the table for him, throwing it out indifferently when it was left uneaten. Watching her sleep, tending the fire or brooding, he felt the outrage of her denial. His conquest of her body should have brought submission, escape, revenge, gradual conciliation—change of some sort—not refuge in her unfailing imperviousness. She had gelded him without giving him a eunuch's compensations. Sometimes, tormented by frustration, he took her brutally, more often he approached her with tenderness and deference, only to be frenzied into ruthlessness by her apathy.

Finally he knew she was with child. He became slavish in his anxiety, his solicitude, his devotion. He tried to care for her, to watch over her food, her rest, her exertions. She submitted to his attentions when it was unavoidable, she showed no pleasure or gratitude. Swollen, she moved slowly, lay from meal to meal on the couch with her eyes open.

He stayed close to the temple, hurrying back from his errands, resisting the temptation to explore the island. When the child was born he would bathe it in warmed water, wrap it in soft leaves, cover it with the furs. After the birth some way of reconciling himself to her would be miraculously revealed, she would speak, he would discover a means of communicating with her people and reviving them. He would cherish the child, protect, nourish, develop, teach, encourage it; it would be the means of establishing himself not only with her but with this place.

A somber, thought-cloying dread hung upon his mind. He walked warily, glancing frequently over his shoulder. If she wanted to leave the temple there was nothing to stop her; so soon as she had grown tall enough to get down from the couch by herself she could have walked away. He knew she would not go yet he feared to find her gone; always when he returned it was a shocking relief that she was there. He babbled to her at length of his apprehensions, he prayed her to assure him she would change, would relent after she bore his child—that nothing would part them.

While she slept he put his hand timidly on her belly and felt the life in it. The thought excited him; he was ashamed of his excitement. He knelt beside the couch to touch her knees and thighs in selfless purity. He kissed her hands, her temples, her hair; when she stirred and frowned, he retreated, hoping she would not waken.

She was near to labor when he heard the shouts and the clang of metal against metal. He ran to her, ready to protect her and the child with his life. She moved away, always keeping a space between them. No one coming upon them could imagine she wanted his assistance or that he had established any right to offer it.

The barbarians burst into sight, waving swords, holding their round shields high above their heads. Their crooked teeth flashed, their mouths opened in wild yells, their rough garments flew back to show their coarse, hairy bodies.

He tried to pull her with him, to lift her in his arms and carry her outside. She resisted obstinately, fiercely, desperately, clinging to the couch, to the table, showing to the full the revulsion and hate in her eyes.

The invaders passed the open side of the temple; Lampley could not believe they had failed to see it or that it hadn't excited their curiosity. Yet they did not turn aside; incredible or not, they were saved. The last one was out of sight when the woman screamed.

He clapped his hand over her mouth; the barbarians came from the side he had let the vines overrun again, cleaving their way through, trampling out the fire, smashing the water gourd, scattering the latest gifts he had brought. They saw and came at him, pointing their weapons so that he could see the faint kinks in the crudely forged steel. He tried to stay, willed himself to meet the swords' edge. Only when she threw her arms around the foremost warrior, offering her ripe belly to his blade, casting a triumphant, malignant look in Lampley's direction, did he finally give in and fly.

CHAPTER FIVE

HE ran through the woods, clamor of pursuit close behind. He headed straight for the lake, remembered he had moved the boat, changed direction. He twisted and turned, hoping to deceive them; they stayed on his heels, gaining, gaining. He reached the shore and plunged into the water. He was not a good swimmer but the current carried him to the beach where the boat was while the pursuers had to turn inland to bypass a thick copse.

He splashed inshore, reaching the boat barely ahead of them. They swarmed at him as he stumbled, pushed the boat into the water with a violent shove and clung to the bow's protection against the rocks they hurled. The missiles splashed close but soon the current took him out of range. With immense difficulty he got himself aboard, and rowed to the opposite shore with his eyes fixed on the island.

It occurred to him that he must be headed directly for the swamp where he had seen the yellow swans. He changed direction; after pulling steadily at the oars, the keel grated on something hard and unyielding. He shivered at the coldness of the air and saw he had grounded at the mouth of a small glacier embedded between rocky hills. He dressed; leaving the boat high on the gravel bordering the ice, he began walking along the shore. The island was far, far away, mistily lilac in the distance, lost and irretrievable.

His shoes, so unaccustomed, spurned and slipped on the gravel and the rocks, floundered in the sand. The chilling wind from the glacier slapped at his back.

Ahead trees-stunted, thick-growing, crowded by underbrush—came down to the water's edge. He pushed through touching branches into still denser thickets, forcing his way against increasing resistance, being forced in turn further and further inland.

Where the tangled growth ended abruptly there was no grass, only stony shale interrupted by ragged shrubs, scanty snowdrifts, bent, leafless trees. Inconstant winds eddied around him, stinging his face, pulling at his clothes, tearing loose twigs from the trees, dead leaves and chaff from the ground, whirling them upward, driving them before it, allowing them to settle only to scatter them again for new torments. He trudged on, head down, walled from the lake— not a glimpse, a fleeting glimpse of the island—climbing, descending, detouring, making he knew not what scant advance.

Advance to where, to what? In an unknown direction to an unknown destination. Nothing could be more stupid; the intelligent thing to do was stop, refuse to go farther. But stop himself, he couldn't.

He stumbled into a valley between gloomy cliffs. There was no vegetation here save sinewy creepers, which seemed to spring directly from the harsh ground, their roots mercifully hidden. They wound and tangled, twisting and untwisting, ever seeking something to climb. He tripped on them, righted himself hastily, fearful that if he fell they would choke him, hold him fast before he could rise. Small dun-colored birds fluttered through them, pecking haphazardly at unseen insects, rose in unsteady, uncertain flight only to settle again a few yards away. He fell; terrified, he scrambled up, shaking himself loose, not really believing the vines had let him go.

He looked up at the far off peaks. What had they to offer him? Romantic towers, magic fastnesses, mystic havens? Cold, craggy, misery. He trod carefully between the vines; perhaps he could reach the next hill before they tripped him once again.

He heard an angry, outraged, murderous squealing and grunting as a horde of wild boars, tiny eyes half-closed, tusks glinting with saliva, shaggy bristles standing out, charged with pounding hooves. He was directly in their path, there was no shelter he could take, and it was clearly useless to run.

He waited, quaking, as they came closer. The foremost animal, the leader, the most ferocious, became enmeshed in the loose vines and began struggling and jerking. His companions shouldered, shoved, worried and bit him; those behind attacked the ones in front. They fell upon their stupefied leader tore him to pieces and devoured him. Then those who chanced to be bitten or slashed were treated the same way, finally those who had merely been blood spattered.

Lampley ran from the scene and splashed through a wide stream he hoped would at least deter the frantic beasts. He climbed over sticky clayish plants with long, tongue-like petals pulling and sucking at his shoes, and bloated grass whose watery blades split apart under his weight, giving out vile fumes to make him sick and giddy. On a rise he looked back at the boars, milling in directionless knots. Far beyond he caught brief, elusive sight of the lake and island. Reluctantly he started up a spur bare of all vegetation, grim and desolate.

The yellowish rock on which he trod was smooth and firm underfoot at first; he climbed over a ridge and began a fairly easy ascent of an escarpment biting into the mountainside. The hard rock gave way to brittle, friable material that broke and crushed underfoot. He came to outcroppings, miniature buttes, which crumbled and rolled at a touch. He found himself walking in a mass of shifting stone, loose and unpredictable.

Ahead, the slope became a series of shoulder-high cliffs, mounting like steps. Very carefully he approached the first and put his hands on the edges to pull himself up. The rock disintegrated under his fingers. He stretched his arms forward and tried to lever himself up with his elbows. The entire face broke off to go gliding and tumbling past him.

He was too far up to retreat and seek a less treacherous way, the best he could do was strike out for the adjoining ridge. He moved cautiously but the strata seemed to shift so that he was faced by a palisade high as his head. He reached up to grasp the ledge. It too split and shattered. He looked in vain for an easier ascent or a crevice where he could work his way up.

Now the cliff towered over him, far above his reach, menacing, sullen. He followed it, searching for a place where it was lower. His feet slipped on the loose stone; it was like walking on marbles. He tried to run, to defeat the restlessness of the rock by speed. His ankle turned; pain and weakness fought each other; he became part of a plunging, toppling, sinking, downward slide, with gravel, debris and boulders crashing around him. The only way he could keep his feet was to run with the avalanche, to embrace the illusion that he was surfboard riding. By a tremendous effort he retained his balance.

He knew it was impossible for him to survive; he must resign himself to being crushed and buried under the landslide. It was pointless to protect his head with his arms as he was doing, it was pointless to run at all. His mind surrendered, only his body continued to fight against destruction. He could not believe his mind didn't really know fear; at a point like this communication was cut off; instincts and reflexes took over.

The roar of the fall became a rumble and then a crackle diminishing into silence as the last fragments rolled and settled. He was almost at the mountain's foot, in a sort of natural quarry hemmed in by palisades on three sides, open only the way he had come down—and this was paved with loose stones in uneasy disarray. It was impossible to scale the sheer cliffs; even at the risk of causing another avalanche he had to go back. Cautiously he began the ascent. Though the rocks turned and shifted under his feet they did not crumble. Picking his way with exaggerated lightness he covered perhaps a hundred, a hundred and fifty feet. He began to hope he might reach a point where he could strike out and away from the incohesive slope.

With a loud report a rock shot from the palisades behind him, arched over his head to crash in front and come bounding down toward him. He jumped aside. It tumbled all the way to the foot of the precipice. From near where it landed another stone discharged itself to fall just behind him. While it was still moving, a ragged bombardment from all three sides began, increasing in intensity till the air was filled with missiles. Fresh slides were started by their impact; the entire mountainside seemed to be converging on him with varying speeds, diving and plunging, lurching and sprawling.

He crouched and cowered. An immense chunk shattered nearby, showering particles and dust.

The palisades erupted in staccato explosions, echoed when the projectiles hit the slide and increased its velocity. He was shaken to realize that the rocks were sentient, individually or collectively, and he was their intended target rather than an endangered spectator. He was doomed; though they missed him a hundred, a thousand times, on the hundred and first or the thousand and first, chance would expose him, make him vulnerable, destroy him. Even if the ground held firm he could not climb out of range before he was felled. And the ground was not holding firm.

There was no escape; who could control the unswerving malice of the rocks? Who indeed? Suddenly he stood erect and held up three fingers in the sign of the letter Shin, the initial of the name Shaddai.

Instantly the mountainside became still. Birds soared overhead, grass sprouted through the rubble and in the crevices of the rocks, clear brooks wound sinuously from the mountaintop, lizards basked on flat spaces, insects moved speculatively from object to object, sheep wandered in search of food.

He threw himself down on a bed of ferns, newly sprung into life. The soft, spiraling ends of the fronds touched his cheeks and hands gently. He moved guardedly, unwilling to crush the tender stems. Raising himself on his elbows he peered down at the pale, feathery snails, the stiff, spotted leaves, the hairy stalks. His throat tightened with wonder and gratitude.

He got up, walked slowly over the solid ground. When he had climbed higher than the palisades he struck out for a plateau, bare of vegetation but not desolate. Shallow ponds sparkled, crystal pinnacles glittered, mounds of quartz reflected the light.   Snakes and crocodiles, strange and nameless reptiles in bright, jeweled colors moved smoothly out of his path. A tinted mist rose from one of the ponds, taking the shape of Mattie. All the women he had known showed themselves in wisps and shreds of vapor. Some were laughing, some wistful, pleading, tempting; all dissolved as fast as they formed. He fled.

He fled from the plain into a forest where leaves made an umbrella against the light, through fields where grain was turning black, past rutted gray roads and decaying rail fences. He passed clumps of berry bushes, bare of fruit, whose thorns raked his hands and face. He stumbled over plowed furrows where the dried clods were woven together with spider webs and made his way through harrowed fields where the exact lines were blurred by rebellious weeds, rooted at random.

The air was cold, colder even than at the glacier, and the light hazier, as though too far from its source. Weeds were persistent, but colorless and sickly. His foot came against something harder than the dry earth; he kicked the weeds aside to reveal a railroad track, crusted and pimpled with rust. There were two tracks, eight, twelve, twenty, an inestimable parallel multitude of them, the steel flaking, the ties rotted, the spikes and plates worked loose. He walked between them.

The skeleton of a model T Ford stood crosswise on the rails. The body was gone, and the hood; the brass radiator, capless, had turned green and brown. A wooden box was athwart the chassis in place of a seat, its ends sticking out over both sides. The tires were flat and shredded.

Lampley lifted the front end and shifted it so that it headed along the right-o-way. He turned the ignition key, pulled down the gas lever, stood in front of the radiator, pulled the choke wire and twirled the crank several times. Then he went back and sat on the box, but not under the steering wheel.

The motor coughed and started, the engine missed in syncopated rhythm, shaking and rattling the frame, failing and fading, catching again. The car bumped slowly over the ties. The Governor, satisfied, made no move to take the wheel. The tracks came together in a series of multiple switches. The Ford stopped, the motor clanked and quit, steam spouted up from the radiator.

Lampley got out. The surface of the rails was no longer rusty but bright with wear. The ties were new, reeking with fresh creosote. They were too close together for his stride; he walked partly on them, partly on the roadbed.

The single diesel car panted on a siding, its garish paint fleeted and peeling. He climbed aboard, walked between the rows of plush-covered seats to the front. The clerk sat in the cab, reading a comic book. He nodded when he saw Lampley. "Board," he shouted. "Aw-aboooooooard!"

The diesel started smoothly. The Governor sat down just behind the clerk and looked out the window. They were running through a Petrified Forest. Some of the trees were riven down the middle, showing the dark, livid heart, the gleaming saffron sapwood, the red-brown bark. Fallen trunks lay in shallow oil, black, broken by lurid rainbows. The car heeled over slightly as it rounded a curve, then more steeply on the opposite side as it picked up speed and took another.

The clerk said, "The island under the world, ay? Good or bad?"

"You can't simplify like that," protested the Governor.

"Can't I? Some law?"

"I mean..."

"Of course you do, of course you do. Enjoy the fishing?"

Lampley saw again the brilliant creatures he had pulled from the lake. "I only caught what was necessary for food," he muttered defensively.

"Necessity is the mother of convention," sighed the clerk; "necessity is the mother of conception, of prevention. Also correction, election, protection, vivisection, selection and so forth. Never perfection."

"Ah," said the Governor, thinking of the woman.

The clerk swung a handle, pulled a throttle, pushed a button. The coach was filled with whirling sparks and balls of fire. "Necessity is the mother of pretension," he sang operatically. A duststorm gathered outside the window, grit forced its way in. The car gained further momentum, swayed and rocked.

"Do we have to go so fast?" asked Lampley.

"Necessity is the mother of dissension and projection. The faster we go, the less room for argument."

The car seemed to be skimming above the rails. The clerk pressed all the buttons in front of him. A pornographic picture was projected on a three dimensional screen. Lightning flashed all around. The comic book, which the clerk had negligently dropped, flamed up and was reduced to curling char. The wind outside roared with hurricane velocity. There was nothing to see through the window but the lumps of earth the storm picked up and held in suspension.

The landscape twinkled into a tunnel, black and close and sooty. The tunnel spiraled upward; the diesel slowed, barely kept from slipping back on the grade. The dark sides gave way to illuminated bas-reliefs showing sphinxes and dragons pursued by hunters with spears and bows; pyramids on which victims were sacrificed with obsidian knives; battles between miniature figures in green or red against others in white or blue while their commanders rode back and forth waving microscopic swords; tableaus of unearthly quietness where boats were poled up wide, muddy rivers flowing through empty prairies.

The tunnel became black again; frigid cold swept through the coach. Icicles formed on the ceiling, frost obscured the windows in flat withes woven together. Lampley shivered so hard he became slightly sick to his stomach. He drew his jacket tight, hugging his chest, trying to control his chattering teeth. The clerk left the cab and built a fire in the aisle. He ripped out seats and fed them to the blaze. By the time the coach was bare the frost-ferns were melting from the windows.

The clerk spun a crank; the light inside turned blue. He hauled a lever back, it changed to green. He jabbed a button; the interior became dark. Lampley saw they were moving smoothly into a terminal, with redcaps running alongside on the platforms. "All out," shouted the clerk. "Change here for North and South, East and West. All out!"

Lampley stood on the platform. "Carry your baggage, sir?" asked a porter

"Sorry, I don't have any," apologized the Governor.

The porter's dark face showed his disbelief. "Everyone has baggage."

"But I don't," insisted Lampley.

"You're trying to cheat a poor man," said the porter. "You're trying to cheat society. You're trying to cheat yourself. Even trying to cheat God."

"Believe me. I'm innocent," cried the Governor.

Loudspeakers bellowed, "Innocent! Innocent!" Far-off cold echoes sounded stonily, "...cent ahahaha...cent ahahaha..." Lights winked on and off. The porter prostrated himself on the platform. An unseen band blared

The Stars and Stripes Forever, firecrackers and rockets went off, a phosphorescent display spelled out KISS ME KID, a barrel rolled and bumped to a stop, disgorging clowns who began tumbling, somersaulting, standing on each other's shoulders to form a cluster reaching to the arched roof where the top man wrote in white chalk on the smoky vault, DRINK MOXIE.

Lampley stood undecided, then walked briskly to the waiting-room. Its chrome and plastic benches were empty, the space between them was filled with robots busily burnishing each other's metal, adjusting each other's mechanism, screwing and unscrewing visiplates, audio systems, sensitizers, olfactometers. He saw no humans. He paused at the unattended newsstand to look over the tattered, smudged periodicals. Journal of Subatomic Medicine. *The Martian Monthly. Space News. Androids Review combined with The Magazine for Mechanical Men Astronomer & Astrogator. Time-Travel Tribune.* There was nothing here to interest him.

Outside the waiting-room he came to the subway stairs, gleaming in white and nickel. They led to an underpass; he could hear the trains rumbling and thundering overhead. He followed the passage to the station; the empty tracks emerged, plunged on into darkness. He sat on a bench; no train came.

He got up and walked along the platform. It went deeper and deeper into the tunnel without narrowing to an end. He came to a place where the tracks were boarded over with heavy planks, flush with the concrete on which he walked. On the other side of the boardwalk small shops offered their wares in dusty, ill-lit windows.

The nearest displayed boots and shoes, sandals, clogs, getas, slippers, moccasins, greaves, buskins, gaiters, spats, wellingtons, overlapping damascene plates to protect the feet of the well-shod knight. All were in sets of threes: right, left, interpediate. The Governor entered; the salesman, dressed in black, hurried to him, rubbing his black-gloved hands together. "Why are all your shoes in triples?" Lampley asked.

The salesman opened his eyes in surprise. "How else would they be.?"

"In pairs, naturally."

"But my dear sir, there's nothing natural about that. Of course there are poor afflicted creatures with only two feet; for them we recommend a very fine prosthetic craftsman who also supplies artificial ears and natural-looking uvulas. But normal persons will find themselves well served here, I assure you. Well-served indeed." He pursed his mouth and looked at Lampley with a combination of severity and servility.

"It—it's all relative, then?" faltered the Governor.

The salesman shrieked. "You monster, you fiend, yea horror! Begone! Begone, I say!"

Lampley closed the door behind him. The next shop was a tobacconist-stationery-novelty store. In the showcase were giant pipes, twists of burley, packages of latakia and perique, warped boxes of dried-out cigars, false mustaches, lapel flowers to spray water in startled eyes, puzzles, cryptograms, tiny spheres fitting endlessly inside of each other, moldering reams of paper, flyspecked envelopes, faded typewriter ribbons, filing indices in Cyrillic. The Governor was not surprised to see the storekeeper was the legless sailor-juggler.

"Come in, lad; a hearty welcome to you," he said. "Been traveling in strange parts, I see. How are the women?"

"Small," said the Governor.

The juggler smacked his thigh with a big hand. He laughed till he coughed. He strapped on a pair of aluminum legs and danced a hornpipe. He took a gallon jug from behind the counter and tilted it against his lips. "Small, ay? Small and naked and full of bile?"

The Governor nodded.

"Then you're poisoned, lad," said the juggler heartily. "You'll never be happy with the other kind again. O the lovelies, the darlings, the dainty morsels: they'll cut out your heart, eat your liver, pluck your eyeballs from your skull, bless them."

"But," said Lampley, distressed, "surely it doesn't have to be that way?"

"Surely, surely," said the juggler.

Lampley bit his lip. "How does one get out of here?"

"Hush," cautioned the juggler. "I have a map. It was traced by the seventh son of a seventh son and lent me under the strictest pledge of secrecy, sealed in black goat's blood. Come along with me." He led the way to the back of the store, through a passage papered in bright orange, the sheets curling apart at the edges where the glue had dried. It was barely wide enough to squeeze through sideways.

The room was triangular, with a pile of brass cogwheels in the narrowest corner. A set of bookshelves sagged against one wall. Calf-bound folios leaned on spiral-backed notebooks. In disorder on top was a collection of papers. The juggler reached among them and took out a thick roll tied with withered pink tape. "Here," he whispered. "Read it and memorize it. Never say who showed it to you."

The Governor unrolled the map. It showed an unfamiliar, an unlikely, a visionary coast. Mermaids and dolphins frisked in the seas; the shoreline was blank, labeled *Terra incognita inferioris.*

"Guess that will fix you up, ay lad?" boomed the juggler. "It's not everybody I'd show it to."

"I'm sure of that," said Lampley. "Thank you."

"Just don't let on to anybody," cautioned the juggler. "Not even if they torture you for it."

"I won't," promised Lampley.

"Think of me," begged the juggler. "Pray for me."

The Governor did not investigate the third shop. He walked past it to the ramp leading to the street. Outside the station the roof of the city pressed down so close buildings of four stories barely cleared it. The street was wide and paved with cobblestones; brilliant copper trolley wires ran overhead.

The city was familiar to Lampley, he had lived in it, knew the names of its quarters and districts. He began walking toward the harbor, the picture of it forming before him, the dark olive water, the black ships suddenly looming up, the tiny figures on the docks, the slowly creaking pilings. The harbor was miles away; miles and miles and miles away.

He passed block after block of gray stone, massive, empty somber buildings. A skeleton came out of one and thrust a dented tin cup before him. The Governor dropped in a coin. It went through the cup and rolled into a gutter running with chaff-flecked dirty water. The skeleton got down on its hands and knee bones to search for it.

A streetcar, royal blue, creaked and whined by. Lampley knew it was headed for the docks also, its passengers stevedores and sailors. A green trolley passed it going in the opposite direction. The motormen saluted each other by clanging their bells in the beat of *Old Black Joe*.

Lampley passed under a gray stone arch spanning the street from building to building. Atop the arch were severed heads of a bear, camel, dog, elephant, ox, weasel. He dropped a coin in the slot and twirled a prayer-wheel set up here to help speed the decapitated creatures to a new incarnation.

Beyond the arch, klieg lights focused on a supermarket. Like the street, it was deserted. The endless shelves held empty cans, their ragged lids sticking cockily upward. The refrigerators were crowded with milk and pop bottles with nothing in them. Unattended cash registers rang NO SALE over and over. Vegetable bins contained carrot tops, potato peels, orange skins, apple cores, cherry stones, peach pits, bean strings, pea-pods, squash seeds, melon rinds. At the butcher counter cellophane bags of fat, gristle, bones and sinews were neatly stacked between trays of clamshells, fish scales, frogs' heads, chicken beaks. Lampley walked on.

He came to a cross street with an arc lamp on each corner—white, violet, gray, reaching into the blackness. He knew it was always night in this city, and he thought of the hundreds of thousands of its inhabitants who worked by day, condemned to a bedridden, insomniac existence. A red streetcar clattered through the intersection, the wires overhead throwing long, shattering sparks as the trolley wheel hit the break, reconnected, glided on.

In the next block there was a cellar with a sign COAL & ICE. The cellar was lit. The Governor peered down at a griffin, its wings folded neatly back, its arrowhead tail tucked away, shoveling crushed ice into a roaring furnace, pausing only to fill a refrigerator with dusty lumps of coal. The building, which housed the cellar, was divided by a lane that descended in long, shallow, stone-flagged steps. This arcade was lined with booths, small and open. Some contained iron-white enameled beds with coverlets thrown back to show wrinkled sheets and indented pillows, barber-chairs adjusted for immediate occupancy, office desks with letters and forms lying on them, bar stools drawn cozily up to bamboo counters, mechanical pants-pressers steaming, open and ready to crease a pair of trousers. There were booths of sheepskins and parchments with the laureate's name blank, certifying every known degree and honor. There were others containing family bibles and photograph albums, dining tables set with silver and napery, bathtubs full of hot water on whose surface floated cakes of soap and scrubbing brushes.

He came to the end of the arcade and stood at another wide street, listening to the night noises of the city. A yellow streetcar stopped beside him. The Governor climbed aboard. There was no conductor, no passengers, no motorman. The straw seats were misshapen, cracked and bristly but the brass work on them and the doors and windows was all fresh and polished. He walked to the front of the car. The sign above his head read .VA TTAW AIV YAWOAT :OWT. He jerked the control knob over the graduated notches. The car bucketed along the street.

The street became two streets, encircling a great, round building whose hundreds of mean and mocking windows were heavily barred. In front of the building was an imposing statue, carved in the same gray stone used throughout the city. Inside the prison were thousands of wretches, dirty, scabby, verminous, starving; thousands of convicts pacing, twitching, planning, calculating, remembering; thousands of convicts behind bland walls, condemned to smell their own bodies and the caustic chemicals, to feed on themselves and refuse, on hate, despair, foolish slyness.

The Governor left the car and beat his hands against the prison. He shouted defiance at the warden, the guards, turnkeys, stoolpigeons, trustees within. He picked up a piece of chalk and tried to write on the impervious, rugged stone. The chalk crumbled before he got beyond FR.

Outraged past bearing, he turned away, brushed by the statue. The figure was two stories high. On the base the letters stood out, shadowed by the streetlights. GOVERNOR ALMON LAMPLEY. He ran back to the car as though pursued, his heart beating anxiously. He swung the knob; the car rattled between empty warehouses, lonesome flats, deserted homes. The arc lights here were a deeper violet, the paving-stones took on a greenish tinge.

He entered the quarter where the foreign consulates were, each with its coat-of-arms carefully emblazoned above the doorway, the flagstaffs bare, windowpanes shattered and broken. After them came professional offices in houses hesitating between being homes or not-homes: dentists, pimps, doctors, mediums, occultists, fortunetellers, literary agents, optometrists, dowsers, narcotics peddlers, osteopaths, contest-promoters, burglars, chiropractors, librarians, counterfeiters, attorneys, tea-tasters, educators, graphologists, architects, lapidaries, phrenologists.

He came to where narrow shops hunched against each other, none with entrances, each with a window for their shop-worn, mildewed goods: the folds of cloth faded and dingy, the hardware corroded and rusty, the books brittle and dog-eared, the bottles fallen and crazed. He passed theaters where marquees, caught between changes, spelled out unintelligible attractions, created hermaphrodite stars. He passed filling stations with hoseless pumps, radio-towers without antennae.

He took the trolley through quiet, quiet streets where all the homes spoke with assurance of sleepers within, of babies fed and diapered, dry and unprotesting, of adolescents on their stomachs and young girls curled into knots, of lovers lying face to face and married couples back to back. He passed shuttered houses, and those with the front door opened in welcome; houses with the porch light left on for the expected visitor, and houses heavy with gloom and repulse. He passed open spaces: vacant lots, cramped parks, areas being excavated.

The street entered a more modern part of the city. The buildings were still of gray stone but here it was more smoothly, more fashionably dressed. There was not one that didn't reach to the roof of the city or embody the horizontal lines of the currently popular style. He halted the car before the department store, which alone thrust its height through the city's enclosing shell and rose, who knew how many stories above it.

It had been remodeled over and over again yet it was still familiar to Lampley as the rest of the city: gray, massive, frowning. Oil lamps with dented reflectors behind them illuminated the show-windows. The Governor reached up and wound the route sign till it read, .HTUOM HTOMMAM-MUTOT XOV :TIAW. He lifted the control handle from its square nut and stuck it in the conductor's coin box. He swung down the steps and stood under the portico of the store, gazing into each window in turn.

One displayed a single egg on a pedestal draped in black velvet that had turned green and purple. Another contained burred screws, threadless bolts, spectacles and eyeglasses with important parts lacking. In the next, women washed clothes in galvanized tubs, scrubbing them against metal washboards, ironing them with sadirons. One of them, stringy gray hair lank on fat shoulders, came forward and pressed her open mouth, like a pig's snout, against the glass. Her teeth were long and jagged, her tongue pale and coated, the inside of her lips spotted with sores. She pulled up her draggled skirt to reveal bunion-shaped shoes and wrinkled black stockings, dancing with bumps and grinds.

He moved slowly past the window crammed with foxed lithographs, broken crockery, disabled bedsprings, a garbage can where a banana lolled from under the lid like a dog's tongue, to the window where a dentist, aided by an ingenious arrangement of mirrors, drilled his own teeth. At intervals he paused, drew a hypodermic needle from his pants pocket and squirted at a canvas on an easel. The artist who stood idly beating a mahl-stick against an open palm, leapt to the easel, working furiously until the paint discharged from the syringe was used up, then sank back into lethargy till the act was repeated and he had a fresh batch of color to use. He was painting a picture of Almon Lampley in track clothes, running for office.

Instead of a revolving door at the entrance there was a merry-go-round. The Governor stepped aboard and bestrode one of the horses, thrusting his feet into stirrups, which were too short and brought his knees too high. The wooden steed, instead of moving gracefully up and down in time to the music of the calliope, bucked and reared. Lampley was glad to dismount and cling to a brass pole. A figure in motorman's uniform—the Governor knew it was his yellow streetcar he had driven—climbed aboard briskly and began collecting fares. He wore a monocle in his left eye on which was etched the island under the earth as seen from the farther shore.

"I'm only trying to get into the store," explained the Governor, unwilling to pay.

"The store. To be sure," said the motorman, as though he had just realized what was beyond the carrousel. "History, ethics, philology, chemistry, geography, heraldry, propaganda, celestial mechanics? A streamlined, up-to-date, late model, trouble-free, labor-saving philosophers' stone? How about the small, extravagant pocket-size for a willion gold moidores? Right now I'm offered a willion; who'll step up and say a stillion, a crillion—a fillion even? Come now, my dear ladies and gentlemen, horses, giraffes (camelopards, if you prefer), ostriches and zebras, surely a fillion moidores is little enough for a love-magnet, a cap of invisibility, or a bottomless purse? Let me hear a fillion. Going once, going twice, going up?"

The calliope played, *In the Good Old Summertime.* "Going up," said Lampley firmly.

"Ah," muttered the motorman, hanging his head. "I was afraid of that." He removed the monocle and crushed it under his heel. The eye behind it was glass. The merry-go-round tilted, sliding Lampley off onto a floor of absorbent cotton sprinkled with tinsel flakes. The calliope switched to *It Had to Be You.* Two Santa Clauses arrived, lugging a barrel. They grasped Lampley under his arms and shoved him into the barrel, jamming his knees against his chest. They rolled the barrel along the floor and up an incline, then they righted it. The staves opened like a flower. Lampley stood erect on the bed of a horse-drawn wagon. The store was full of wax dummies engaged in copulation.

A top hatted, nightshirted man on stilts marched through, carrying a pickaxe over his shoulder. He attacked a section of the wall with the pick. After a few strokes water gushed forth, sweeping the dummies away. The man took a blowtorch from under his hat and froze the water on the floor. A motion-picture projector threw colored images of fleecy blue and pink clouds. An organ played *O Promise Me* (pianissimo) while handholding couples skated tirelessly over the ice.

The Governor jumped from the wagon, and avoiding the irregular edges of the ice, walked quickly over to the stationery department. A mahout in turban and loincloth pecked at the keys of a typewriter with his goad. Each time the machine came to the end of a line a balloon emerged from the side, inflated slowly, floated up out of sight. Lampley cleared his throat. "Could you tell me the way to the elevators?"

The mahout whacked the typewriter furiously with his goad. Balloons issued like bubbles in an aquarium tank. They clustered together in midair to spell WHATEVER GOES DOWN COMES UP. Lampley spied a floorwalker doing a handstand on a cash register. "Could you—" he began.

The floorwalker sprang down nimbly, folding his arms. He took the carnation from his buttonhole and held it between his teeth. He punched the keys of the register. Three plums appeared. He punched them again; four lemons jumped into sight. He rang up, IOUOI. He handed the receipt slip to the Governor with a low bow. It read, THE AMOUNT OF YOUR PURCHASE IS $00.00. THANK YOU; YOU ARE ENTITLED TO A REFUND. Lampley turned it over. On the other side was printed, YOUR WEIGHT IS 181 POUNDS. YOU WILL BE LUCKY IF YOU AVOID.

The Governor dropped the card and went to the bank of elevators. The doors slammed open, one of the clowns he had seen at the terminal stuck his head out. "Foreign tongues, quartermelons, odd fish, rooterbeggars, soft hearts, hot potatoes, proud flesh, birds of a feather, prime movers, mustrooms, red herrings! Going GUP!"

"Please," said the Governor.

The clown opened his painted mouth and wabbled it. Then he fell out of the elevator on his face. Lampley stepped around him into the cage. The clown picked himself up, his feet slipping from under him again, threatening a pratfall, so that he had to keep his legs whirling to maintain balance. He sneezed. His mask flew off to uncover the clerk's face.

"You're keeping the doctor waiting; hurry, hurry, hurry." He closed the door, snapped it open. "Out," he said sternly, threatening the Governor with one of his clown's flapping shoes.

CHAPTER SIX

THE vaulted ceiling of the windowless waiting room was upheld by Romanesque pillars. It was so low Lampley could have touched it without stretching his arms to the full. Dirt had worked its way into every unevenness of the whitewashed surface. Unshaded bulbs stabbed his eyes. A girl sat in an armchair, rolling and unrolling a magazine. A woman in her thirties pulled at her glossy black hair; when a strand came loose she tucked it back under her hat, then pulled at it again. A row of plastic mannequins, smiling, dressed in blouses and hats with veils but skirtless and unshod, were wedged tightly together on a long bench. The Governor looked for a vacant seat; there was none.

The thick whitewash on the ceiling and pillars constantly flaked off, falling in a fine, dusty powder on the limp carpet, to be trodden by nervous feet. Lampley scraped a short semicircle with the toe of his shoe; the layer was very deep. A mouse came out of the wall and stood in the middle of the floor. No one paid any attention. A white cat with black and orange patches prowled past, rubbed itself against the Governor's leg, saw the mouse and crouched, tail lashing. The mouse scuttled for its hole; the cat pounced—too late. It mewed pitifully.

An elderly nurse entered the waiting room. Her cap was perched on hair dyed butter yellow, her hound's cheeks had bull's-eyes of rouge on the bones, her down-turned mouth was unevenly lipsticked in raspberry red. "Doctor will see you now," she announced.

The girl and woman jumped up. The nurse walked past them. "Me?" asked Lampley.

She wheeled about; he followed her. The girl took the woman's seat and began fussing with her hair; the woman sank into the girl's chair and rolled the magazine. The dummies' eyes crinkled and winked behind their veils; they had no mouths.

The nurse led him through a cracked and splintered door, the frame eaten by termites and dry rot. She swished her stiff skirt down a hall smelling of anesthetics, dried blood, food cooked and forgotten. The plaster was cracked and bulging, seemingly held in place by the thick, greasy paint. The hall opened on a dressing room with triple-mirrored vanity-table. Cotton smocks of varying lengths hung on hooks. "Put on a gown please," she ordered.

"But I…"

She gave him an arch look. "You wouldn't expect Doctor to do your little work while you had your clothes on, now, would you? Come, dear—there's no use being shy at this stage. And let's not keep Doctor waiting; Doctor's a busy man."

She drew the curtain behind her; it was glossy-green with the word PULLMAN stitched to it. The Governor slowly took off his jacket, tie and shirt. There was a calendar on the wall, a calendar for the year he had gone into politics, after he and Mattie had been married for eighteen months. The picture was of an abnormally short-torsoed girl saying, "Let's have fun!"

Lampley selected the longest gown. It was not only too short, the edges were grimed. He put it on and pulled the curtain aside. The nurse said, "Let's not be nervous, dear. If you'd seen as many as I have come in to have their little work done you wouldn't think any more of it than brushing your teeth. I've had it done myself a dozen or two times. This way, please."

She preceded him into a grim office. Blue skies and flowering trees were painted on the glass of closed windows. There was a gray operating table under floodlights, and an oak desk with mustard-colored streaks. A man with a sharp nose, close-clipped gray mustache, large, cloudy spectacles sat behind the desk, looking over pads, pencils, ashtrays and a portable radio. A wilted rose was thrust into a buttonhole of his nylon smock. Two younger nurses leaned their elbows on the table, intent only on their animated conversation.

"Now then," said the doctor, putting his hands behind his head and tilting back. "Let's take a little case history, shall we?"

"There's nothing wrong with me," stated the Governor.

The younger nurses tittered, the older one patted him on the shoulder. "That's the spirit, dear."

The doctor murmured, "It's just a formality, you know."

"But I don't know," argued the Governor.

The doctor looked annoyed. "Let's not waste time." All three nurses agreed in unison, "Let's not waste Doctor's time. There are twenty girls waiting to have their little work done."

The radio played, *Take Me Out to the Ball Game*.

"Forty," snapped the doctor.

"Forty," echoed the nurses. "Forty girls waiting to have their little work done. If you knew how grateful they were to Doctor, you wouldn't waste Doctor's time."

"But—" began the Governor.

"Enough!" shouted the doctor, standing up. "I can't stand these silly creatures who chop and change."

"Doctor is the only one entitled to chop and change," admonished the elderly nurse.

The doctor came from behind the desk. "Are we ready?"

"Yes, Doctor."

The radio played *Anchors Aweigh*.

"Then let's get it over with." They grabbed his wrists and ankles. He did not struggle. They hoisted him on the table; a needle pierced his arm. "Just relax, dear," advised the elderly nurse.

Lampley grew helpless. He tried to raise his arms; he rolled his eyes. The doctor said, "Nice going. Very nice. Now then."

A frightful stab of pain went through him. Then a worse one, more prolonged, probing, searching. He tried to scream but his mouth wouldn't open, his larynx and diaphragm refused response. The pain was beyond bearing: sharp, hot, slashing, searing through his abdomen, forking through kidneys, lungs, heart, throat.

"Ha-ha, nothing to it," chortled the doctor.

"Not when *you* do it, Doctor," cried all three nurses together.

"Shall we put it under the microscope and see what it was?" asked the doctor jovially.

"Oh, yes, Doctor, do," responded the nurses.

They left him. Lampley felt the blood gushing from the wound in his body, heard the pulse in his neck grow faint. Weakness didn't diminish his pain, only made him less able to bear it. He judged the anesthetic was wearing off; he moved dry tongue against cracked lips. If not for the loss of blood and the drag of pain he might be able to raise his arms, or at least turn his head to see what they were doing.

"A boy," said the doctor. "One little assistant less."

The nurses cackled. "Oh, Doctor, you're so witty. You're a regular killer."

The older nurse came over to the table and took the Governor's hand. "How do we feel?" she inquired perfunctorily, "now our little work is all done?"

Lampley groaned.

"Never better, ay? Well, girls will be girls, I always say. Once you've had your little work done you're good as new till next time. S hall we get dressed now?"

"Wa-water," moaned the Governor.

The radio played a medley of *Jingle Bells, Tea for Two, Smoke Gets in Your Eyes, St. James Infirmary,* and *April Showers.*

"A little water? All right, dear. Just come with me." She helped him off the table without solicitude. The pain came in dull, hard thrusts. His mind crawled in disparate ways, a spider whose legs writhed, though the body had been transfixed. He could move but he had trouble controlling his movements. He put one foot very carefully before the other and leaned on the nurse as she guided him back to the dressing room. "You can rest if you like," she offered brightly. "But not tooooo long, because there are others waiting for their little work. Doctor is a very busy man, you know."

He clutched the edge of the vanity; the face three times reflected in the mirrors was unchanged: the well-groomed, almost handsome, dignified yet twinkling, lightly aged, thoughtful but friendly face of the state's chief executive and first magistrate. He turned away in shame and horror.

Shakily, he got out of the smock, letting it lie in a wrinkled, blood-spotted, ugly pile. He stood, cowering a little, waiting for the agony, the fire inside him, to recede before he slowly, so slowly, put on his clothes. Leaning against the wall, he endured the spasmodic cramps. He saw that the calendar was gone; in its place was the bright cover of a seed catalogue. The curtain was now marked, BOX F.

The hall was a round tunnel pervaded by an overpowering smell. Spiraling ridges, set close together, reflected a dizzying light whose source he could not see. He stooped slightly to avoid the ridges above his head. Walking was awkward but—apart from the pain—not too difficult. He tried to identify the smell, familiar and not unpleasant though strong, but he could not. He put his hand against the grooves, somehow expecting them to be warm and moist; they were dry and cold.

His head brushed the roof, forcing him to crouch. After a short distance he had to stoop still further, then crawl on hands and knees. The peculiar effect of the reflected light—as though he were looking through the inside of a tightly compressed corkscrew—hurt his eyes. He shut them; this only made the pressure against his flesh more noticeable. He opened them again.

He could no longer crawl; he had to wriggle slowly forward. A bright ball of light far ahead dimmed the sinuous windings around him. He was sure it indicated an opening too small for him to get through. He bitterly regretted not having stretched his arms ahead of him while the size of the tunnel still allowed it. He progressed by digging in the toes of his shoes for a forward push, aided by arching his back. His shirt was wet with sweat; jagged flashes shot through his head.

He was exhausted, unable to move farther. The cessation of movement, of effort did not ease him or recruit his strength to go on. He dared not give up, relax, slacken his will. He was condemned to go on and on, to bruise himself against the ever-narrowing passage. The necessity to complete the journey had been ordained before he was born. There was nothing to do but force himself to shrink even more tightly together, to compress his rebellious body into the prescribed space.

The pipe debouched partway up on a wall; the Governor looked down upon a brightly polished floor of inlaid wood. A large area was enclosed within barbed-wire entanglements, guarded by unmanned machine guns. Beyond this area the normal business of the department store proceeded: customers strolled through aisles of merchandise, salespeople waited on them; between the two societies was bare floor.

Inside the wire enclosure tombstones were displayed, voting machines, parking meters, printing presses, atom bombs, wireless masts, garbage trucks, spaceships, oil derricks, semaphores, gas pumps, power shovels, parachutes, purse seins, burglar tools, cyclotrons, glass eyes, a stuffed whale, medals and orders of chivalry and nobility. Closely shaven men in dark blue, dark gray, dark brown suits, neck microphones resting on their hand-painted ties, traded these things to each other—a truck for a net, a medal for a gravestone.

In the exact center of the enclosure, suspended from the ceiling, an electric signboard offered quotations which moved slowly along from right to left, allowing the slowest reader time to grasp them. BONE TOOLS 37⅛...CONSOLIDATED ALCHEMISTS 104...INTERSTELLAR DRIVE PREF 66¼...CSA BONDS #5...UNITED METROPOLITAN HOT CRUMPET & PUNCTUAL DELIVERY LTD 70...

One of the presses began turning, the paper flashing by on the cylinders in an endless stream. As they were spewed out and automatically cut and folded, the headlines were large enough for the Governor to read. LAMPLEY NOMINATED said the top one. A broker seized and stamped on it. GOVERNOR FAILS TO GET NOD read the one below, then in rapid succession, GOVERNOR'S OPPONENTS IN UNITY BID, CONVENTION

DEADLOCK, LAMPLEY SWEEPS PRIMARIES, LAMPLEY SWAMPED IN PRIMARIES, THREE-CORNERED NOVEMBER RACE SEEN.

One of the brokers retrieved LAMPLEY NOMINATED and held up the smudged paper. Someone bid the stuffed whale. They slapped each other on the back, they fell into each other's arms helplessly, they rolled on the floor in ungovernable laughter after putting on coveralls to protect their clothes, they drew revolvers from hip-pockets and shot them into the air, stamping and rollicking in mirth. When delight at the jape finally died down, a broker offered, LAMPLEY SWEEPS PRIMARIES. There were no takers.

The illuminated ticker jerked in its hitherto smooth run. LAMPLEY 41½...DEHYDRATED AARDVARK 88...UNITED ARBALEST & HARQUEBUS 90¼...LAMPLEY 40⅞...MONTGOLFIER AERONAUTICS 284...EAST INDIA CO GE⅜...LAMPLEY 39...SPACE DOGS & GENERAL MUTANTS 368½...ENGLISH CHANNEL TUBE 111...LAMPLEY 37...HERO'S ALEXANDRIA STEAM POWER DEVELOPMENT 104¼...MARTIAN SUBDIVISIONS 208...LAMPLEY 35...

A broker pointed his finger at the Governor. He would have shrunk back; the smallness of the tube forbade it. All the traders lined up and stared at him through binoculars.

The signboard speeded up:

LAMPLEY 32...LAMPLEY 29...LAMPLEY 21...LAMPLEY 14...LAMPLEY 9...LAMPLEY 1...LAMPLEY...

"Yah!" they shouted in chorus. "You'd have to pay us to take you."

"Pay us! Pay us!"

Each put a hand on the shoulder in front. They snake-danced around and between the displays. The signboard began spelling out, BORN IN A HOSPITAL, OF AVERAGE INCOME BUT NOTABLY IMPROVIDENT PARENTS, HE EARLY SHOWED THE APTITUDES CALCULATED TO PUT HIM IN SECOND PLACE AT ALL TIMES. Oil began gushing up through the derricks and splashing on the floor. The smelting furnaces produced gold bricks. The stuffed whale's seams burst to show it was filled with stocks and bonds, promissory notes, mortgages, checks, bank-books and trust deeds. The signboard read, UNIQUE SPECTACLE: GOVERNOR PUFFED WHEAT WILL NOW BE SHOT FROM THE...

He felt the tremendous pressure building up behind him, tried to resist, gave up. The men below stood at attention, their right hands placed reverently against their left breasts. The Governor soared over their heads in a wide arc, above busy departments and dark, still spaces. He found he could control his flight, made a neat immelmann turn, and came gently to rest on a balcony overlooking the florist department. Scent of frangipani, orange blossoms, cereus, honeysuckle, liana floated up to him. Orchids bloomed in midair, lilies blossomed on plants rooted in the grass mats bestrewed over the floor.

The balcony was cluttered with anchor-chains, spool, of telephone conduit, cotton bales, spare parts for mechanical chessplayers. Lampley trod carefully between them and opened a door marked NO ADMITTANCE, SERVICE ONLY, DO NOT ENTER, THIS MEANS YOU. The room had no proper floor, only closely woven flatsteel strips, which sagged at every step. Enlarged X-ray photographs lined the walls; light shone through them to show up the deformed bones like parachutes, like plows, like cutlasses. The clerk, wearing an admiral's gold-laced cocked hat and the black robes of a judge over his blue jeans, sat in a porch swing that swayed gently to and fro behind a pulpit. He looked inquiringly at the Governor.

"Why did you take me to that doctor?" demanded Lampley.

The clerk shrugged and took a pinch of snuff. He sneezed. "Why did you go?"

Lampley pondered. "You forced me," he said at last.

The clerk plucked a dry weed from a candlestick on the pulpit and chewed it thoroughly. "You didn't resist."

"I—I was taken by surprise," stammered Lampley.

"There are no accidents."

"But—"

"And there is free will," affirmed the clerk drowsily, the swing almost stopped.

"I didn't go voluntarily."

The clerk opened his eyes wide. "Mmm. Also mmmmm."

"I—" The Governor was unable to say more.

The clerk stood up in the swing, reaching out his arms to the chains and began pumping with his feet. The swing cleared the pulpit, knocked over the candlestick, which bounced on the steel floor. He let go the chain, folded his arms. The swing subsided into gentle motion. The clerk jumped down and brought up a heavy law book from under the pulpit. He laid it open on the lectern, riffling through it. Several moths flew out from between the pages. "You plead not guilty?" he asked coldly.

"I don't understand."

"Yon plead non compos parentis, in loco ignoramus, ab squatulatis feasance, nolo comprendere?"

"That's nonsense," exclaimed the Governor.

"Certainly. Convicted in the thirty-third degree."

"I demand a suspended sentence."

"Granted," accorded the clerk, lying on the swing again, face down, so that his voice was muffled. "Now then! You insist the responsibility wasn't yours?"

"What's the use of going into that?"

The clerk sat up and adjusted his hat from the Napoleonic tilt it had assumed when he was prone to the proper fore-and-aft position. "The defendant is instructed that evasion is paramount to tutti-frutti. Answer the question or be incontemptible."

"It wasn't my idea," said the Governor sullenly.

"You consented, however."

"I 'consented'? Was she some chattel who needed dispensation from me?"

The clerk shook his finger.

"I actually tried to persuade her not to do it."

The clerk tore several pages out of the book and constructed an airplane. It flew silently over their heads, dropping leaflets a quarter the size of postage stamps. The Governor tried to control his nervous shrinking. "It wasn't as if she were a silly girl. I mean, it was a considered decision on her part—nothing frivolous or vain…"

His voice trailed off. The clerk tore out another page and made a cannon. He shot a wing off the plane with it; the machine whirled down lopsidedly and crashed on the pulpit. "If that's the way you want it, that's the way you want it. Let's go."

"Where to?"

"Ah," said the clerk. "If we only knew." He removed the cocked hat and black robe and dropped them in a wastebasket. He pressed a button on the pulpit, which immediately swung aside to reveal a manhole. A ladder rose out of the depths in short jerks. As it neared the ceiling a trapdoor fell open. The ladder glided through and stopped. "You first," said the clerk.

Lampley climbed the ladder, feeling he might lose his hold on the rungs at any step. When he was almost to the top he looked down. The clerk had disappeared. Carpenters were laying a wooden floor, erecting partitions. Porters removed the swing and the pulpit. Wiring, air-conditioning, telephones, interoffice communication-systems, were installed rapidly. One of the workers took up an ax and began chopping at the ladder.

Lampley climbed through the floor. He was in a court with squat walls, and gateways wider at the bottom than the top, bearing winged suns. He passed between rows of statues, animal-headed gods, men and women wearing conventionalized wigs and beards in stylized poses. The pale light gave the reds, greens and blues, which predominated, a chalky, muffled quality; it threw the looped crosses molded on the frieze into shadowed relief.

The air was dank with the penetrating, pervasive dampness of oozing stone. Lampley was oppressed by thoughts of decay and destruction, of the knowledge without the sensation of pain. He longed for the warmth of the sun outside the hotel or the climate of the island under the earth. He shuddered away from the hidden corners, suggestive of toads and snakes, small animals decomposing and maggotty. This place should have had some measure of sanctity, induced some feelings of reverence or at least contemplation. He was aware only of the sodden air.

He walked moodily from the dusky precincts into the shocking light of a busy office. Girls in tight pink nylon bathing suits, their hair dyed royal blue, wearing blue nail polish, blue lipstick and red eye shadow, sat at transparent plastic desks, inserting thin rectangles of Swiss cheese into tabulating machines. Each desk had a silver champagne ice bucket in which rested a telephone. Beside the machines a row of feather dusters in graduated sizes were arranged in neat holders. Lampley saw pretzels were being used as paper clips.

"Pardon me," he said. "Is this the accounting department?"

The four nearest girls looked up in panic. Alarm bells rang shrilly, rockets popped out of the centers of the feather dusters, fire sprinklers showered down rainbowed sparks. The pretzels unwound limply. The slices of Swiss cheese curled into rolls out of which confetti blew in continuous blasts.

A girl pulled her phone out of the ice bucket and choked herself by winding the cord around and around her throat. The next one reached in her desk for a pair of waterwings, inflated them and began practicing the breaststroke. Others mutely handed him sheaf after sheaf of statements, loading them on his reflexively outstretched arms until the top ones slid off onto the floor. He could see they were made out to him but he had no chance to read the items or prices.

They piled the bills faster and faster; girls came from the farthest desks, staggered under armfuls. He dumped what he was holding and tried to struggle free from the mounting heap but it was already above his waist; he could not get his legs loose. He dug with his hands; the papers slipped down to cram the holes as fast as he dug. They imprisoned him with their weight; first the left, then the right arm was pinned to his side.

Buried to the chin, he filled his lungs with air, foreseeing the covering of his mouth and nose. The pressure was painful now; he felt his ribs slowly caving in. The deluge ceased; the girl who had choked herself wormed her way to him on her belly, creeping up the paper mound, dragging the telephone behind her. She pressed her swollen, twisted, blackened tongue against his lips, looked into his eyes with her protruding glazed ones.

He wrenched his face away. G irls approached with rubber stamps so large they could barely lift the bulbous handles. As they were raised he read DIAP on their dark purple surfaces. The girls hurled and slashed them downward, biting into the bills. With each thump masses of paper vanished. His arms were disengaged, then his legs. He breathed deeply, took a step, leaving only scattered invoices on the floor.

The girls threw themselves at his feet. "Take us," they moaned, "use us, violate us, degrade us. We love you."

The Governor shuddered as he perceived they were all sisters, product of a multiple birth; in each face he saw the features of the strangled girl. The one with the waterwings, using a crawl, swam rapidly between the others and raised her clasped hands imploringly. She was drowning. He rolled her over and began clumsily giving her artificial respiration. Her hair gradually turned white, the blue dye floating in a powdery cloud above her head. He put the valve of the waterwings to her mouth and expressed the air. She opened her eyes.

"Let us go," she said.

The others protested, weeping, clasping and unclasping their hands, tearing at their bathing suits in anguish, clutching their throats in grief, but they did not try to hold him. He helped the white-haired girl to her feet. She drew a key from between her breasts and handed it to him. He put it in his pocket and they left the office. As soon as they were outside her hair changed to brown, the pink bathing suit became white, her nail polish, lipstick and eye-shadow faded. She shivered.

"Are you cold?" She nodded. "We must find something to put around you."

There was no one in sight. This part of the store had an air of neglect, as though it had been used for storage, shut up and forgotten. The showcases looked as though they had been discarded from more enterprising sections; they were of odd sizes, with dull glass, in some cases cracked and repaired. Many were empty, others contained pearls, loose toothpicks, used cartridge cases, false teeth, celluloid collars, oil cans, rare stamps.

They came to an escalator powered by two ponies working a treadmill, and rode to the floor above. A floorwalker in morning clothes, binoculars dangling on his chest from a leather strap, hastened to them. "Customers only, customers only," he barked.

"We're looking for a coat or a cloak," the Governor informed him.

"Nothing but mink or sables here," said the floorwalker coldly, surveying them through the binoculars.

"We'll take either," said Lampley.

The floorwalker knelt and kissed the Governor's shoe. He reached behind him and took the tails of his frockcoat in his fingers and tore it up the back, placing the two halves before their feet. A saleswoman with a diamond collar sparkling on her neck rolled up in a motor scooter. "This way, if you please."

Two grapnels emerged from the scooter and hooked on to the pieces of coat; Lampley and the girl rode them like water skis to a small, shallow auditorium. An old-fashioned carrier system hummed overhead, its wire baskets moving briskly back and forth, disappearing above the proscenium arch of a cramped stage on which models pranced and postured in furs. When they turned rapidly, flirting the cloaks, Lampley saw they wore nothing beneath and that they were all gravid.

"I'll take that one," said the girl, pointing.

The curtain thumped down. The saleswoman pulled a cord on the carrier system. "Madam has excellent taste, for a slut," she complimented the girl. An oversized basket brought the model clutching the cloak tightly about her. She was cowering in terror. The saleswoman pulled the cord again and the basket tipped, tumbling the model out. "Rip it off her back," she ordered.

The model cried out. "Oh, wait. Please wait," she begged.

"You beast," said the saleswoman. "You pretty little female beast. What rights have you? What feelings have you? You were born for this moment."

The model moaned.

"Is there no other way?" asked the Governor.

The saleswoman stared at him. "How could there be? This isn't the place for cheap merchandise or cheap methods." She gave the order again.

The model sank to the floor in a trembling heap. "The poor thing," said the girl in the bathing suit. "Will it hurt her very much?"

"What difference does it make?" asked the saleswoman. "It'll be over before you know it. And there are plenty of other models. All this palaver over a wretched creature! It's disgusting."

"I can't do it," whispered the girl. "I'm too tender-hearted."

"Chicken-hearted, you mean," sneered the woman. "Anyone can see what you are. All right, let him do it then."

"No," said the Governor firmly.

"You'll have to pay just the same," warned the woman.

"Very well." He drew the key from his pocket and handed it to her.

"And take your property with you."

The model walked humbly behind them. "Still cold?" asked Lampley.

"Yes I am. And if you were a gentleman you'd have seen that I got my coat."

He didn't answer. The floorwalker, in a new frockcoat, bowed pleasantly to them and waved them to the elevator. Lampley pressed the button, noting that there was no indicator above, that there never had been indicators over any of the elevator entrances. The thought depressed him.

The doors rolled open. The cage was very large, with wide brown leather benches around three sides, and a padded leather ceiling and walls. The clerk wore a leather jockey cap, and a rawhide vest over his blue jeans. He clasped his hands together over his head as they entered. He closed the doors smartly; the elevator lurched sideways, throwing the girl and model to the benches.

"I hope—" began Lampley.

The clerk nodded. "Excellent, excellent. Where there's hope there's life and where there's life there's despair. A beginning, anyway."

"I meant I hoped—"

"Heard you," said the clerk. "Let's not say the same thing more than once." The car stopped and he opened the doors. Lampley could see nothing clearly through the clouds of steam outside. After a slight hesitation the girl left, followed by the model. The Governor moved after them; the clerk barred his way. "Ladies only," he said politely.

"You weren't so particular at the doctor's office," argued Lampley angrily.

"Yang and Yin," explained the clerk. "Circumstances alter faces."

The elevator shot upward. The noise of airhammers and riveting machines grew loud; it was succeeded by the sounds of distant motors, wind rustling in the trees, surf spuming against rocks, hooves clopping on soft asphalt. "You want out here?" asked the clerk. "Or will you try for a higher number?" Before the Governor could answer, the elevator stopped. Lampley stepped out on linoleum with the pattern worn off, the burlap backing showing through in streaks. A gloomy corridor, warm and fetid, stretched ahead of him. He turned back to the elevator but the doors were shut.

He paced along the corridor, past tarnished spittoons, sagging chairs, earthenware umbrella stands. The saffron wallpaper hung in shaggy strips, spider webs loaded with the dried chitin of insect victims tied it to the pocked plaster. Tarnished metal signs exhorted, NO SMOKING, DON'T SPIT ON THE FLOOR, SILENCE, NO WOMEN ALLOWED, FIREARMS PROHIBITED, ACT LIKE YOUR MOTHER SAW YOU. The light bulbs were the ancient carbon type; their filaments glowed an angry red through the flawed, smeared glass.

He entered a room whose wooden walls were riddled with holes, the remaining surfaces powdery and fragile, reeking with slime and foul smells. Men lay on the floor in their own filth and vomit, their greasy clothes clutched across thin chests, sagging bellies, protruding adams-apples. They quivered and twitched, squirmed and tossed, turned on their sides and then on their backs. They moved their arms under their uneasy heads, rolled over on them, jerked them up. They snored, wheezed, gasped, cried out. They burrowed unshaven faces, heavy with sores, scars, bloody cuts, into their elbows or against hunched shoulders. The Governor picked his way between them as best he could, anxious not to stumble, dreading to touch one of them with his foot.

At the end of the room an alabaster basin, perhaps twenty feet across, was full to the brim with sewage. Gorged and sluggish flies hovered, or lit briefly on bobbing orange-peels.

He shuddered lest some tremor of the floor, some unseen current of air cause the loathsome bog to overflow and reach him.

He finished his cautious tour and entered a circular anteroom whose sides were completely taken up by divans and easychairs upholstered in faded green plush. Gas brackets curved outward from the walls, holding fan-shaped yellow flames like halting palms. A chandelier was suspended from the ceiling, its glass prisms and teardrops reflecting the violet end of the spectrum. Below it was a round settee with a blunted cone of upholstery rising in its center; the seat might have accommodated twenty pairs of buttocks; no more than four shoulders could have found space against the spindling back. This cone supported a cast-iron statuette of an effeminate youth or a mannish girl—it was impossible to tell which because of the chaste metallic drapery. There was no one in the room.

The Governor paused before the halls raying out from the anteroom. They were all precisely alike, shadowed, somber, murky; he chose the center one. The glow of kerosene lamps enshrined in recesses made pale brown half moons on the mud-colored floor. He would not have been surprised had the hall led to some cell from which there was no return, instead it ended in another anteroom. This one was square, with board benches. Fat candles on wooden stands slowly dripped wax; the floor was covered with sawdust and shavings.

There was a row of double-hinged saloon doors reaching from knee to shoulder. Lampley pushed through one. Sleepers were even more numerous here, piled closer together, and their smell was more nauseating. Some of the faces were rigid, lips drawn back in a snarl to uncover noisome caverns. Others were mobile in sleep, grinning, grimacing, teeth-grinding, cheek-puffing. Pale worms crawled out of one open mouth.

He recognized some of the sleepers. Playmates, school fellows, college acquaintances, his first employer, merchants and farmers to whom he had sold tractors or plows, political allies he had left behind, a candidate he had ostensibly supported, a lobbyist to whom he had promised his vote before he changed his mind, a legislator of the same party whom he had disavowed, an office-seeker whom he had praised with calculated faintness—a dozen others. He could remember the names of none. He saw a man he was sure was his uncle, his mother's brother, in whose home he had lived and who had sent him to school. "Uncle—Uncle—" he stammered, but the name would not come. He stooped to rouse the man, to beg him to tell his name, to relieve the burden of forgetfulness. His uncle—if it was—slept on, knees drawn up, jaw slack, fingers fluttering. Lampley's hands fell away from the recumbent figure.

He hooded his eyes against the other faces, heeding only the legs and bodies to keep himself from stumbling. He saw the treasures, tokens, souvenirs, keepsakes the outcasts possessed, spilled from their hands or pockets onto the crowded floor: curling photographs, creased letters, cracked newspaper clippings, locks of lifeless hair, tarnished luckpieces, battered amulets, illegible diplomas, crumpled certificates.

The dormitory was surrounded by bathrooms of lustrous tile, milky porcelain, harsh chrome fixtures. Men slept on the spotless floors, in the immaculate tubs, draped themselves over lavatories and close-stools. The one Lampley entered seemed less crowded than the others. A figure on the floor struggled free of his companions. It was the clerk. He closed the door and twisted the faucet in the bathtub. The elevator shot upward.

"I don't seem to remember any of the names," apologized the Governor.

The clerk smiled tolerantly, then frowned. He turned the faucet hard over; the elevator's speed became frightening. "There's forgetting and forgetting," he said. "Anyway, you'll remember these."

"What?" asked Lampley.

"These," said the clerk. The elevator stopped with a jolt. The clerk waved his hand. "Your floor."

CHAPTER SEVEN

IT WAS a telephone exchange, with minute light-buttons flashing on and off. The switchboards were back-to-back: as the Governor walked slowly along he could see only the operators opposite. They were all girls he remembered poignantly, girls he had loved, whose images had filled his mind, girls he had wanted, courted, thought about through restless nights, girls he had been too timid, too awkward, too shy or inept to have. There was not one whose name or voice or scent he lad forgotten. Sheila, whose spare, tanned body tormented his adolescence, smiled up at him with those tantalizing lips, thin but so perfectly, so sweetly curved. Beth, who swam and sailed and rode like a boy but constantly reminded him she was a girl, waved a free hand as she plugged into the board with the other. And there was Marge, Marge of the translucent skin, and hair the silvery gold of a full moon on a hot summer's night, Marge, whose exquisiteness it had been agony not to touch, hold, crush, raven. They were all there: Anne, Louise, Ellen, Charlotte, Gwen, Dot, Jill, Hermina, Belle, Sybil... All those rewards ironic experience informed him belatedly he could have known. Grief swelled internally; he felt the tears flowing backward from his eyes down to his throat and lungs.

The girls' darting fingers snapped and unsnapped the connections in rapid rhythm. The pointed plugs were rifle bullets growing out of living vines rooted in the switchboards. This was his chance to call Marvin; what if some vital business had come up?

Yet he could not signal to the girls opposite: Connie, whose husband had contributed to his campaign for councilman, Martha, met at some dull affair, who had gotten tight with him. He could not ask them for an impersonal number; he dared not address them familiarly after realizing how fully he had failed them. The telephone exchange was a place where communication was impossible.

His steps slowed; he grudged leaving the women even though he could not reach or touch them, even though he was as helpless to stay as he had been to seduce. His sadness at the implacability of fate merged with a gentler, resigned nostalgia.

The last pair of switchboards was unoccupied. The Governor pulled a plug out from each; the vine-wires were straight and inflexible. They sped through the air, escaping his fingers, growing diagonally upward. Thinner tendrils sprang out from them at intervals and entwined into the rungs of a slanting ladder. Lampley put his foot on the lowest; it was springy but it held his weight without bending too far. He mounted rapidly.

Halfway up he looked back. The vines had sprouted umbrella-sized leaves, making a curtain between him and the exchange. He caught glimpses of blonde, red or brown heads and thought he heard weeping and laughter. Hummingbirds, moths and dragonflies in brilliant colors lit on the foliage; the leaves turned scarlet and orange. Gentle winds rustled them.

The wind on the floor to which he climbed was gray and desolate. Far across the emptiness he saw a twenty-four motored plane being warmed up while the waiting passengers cooled cups of coffee in the wash of the propellers. Equally distant in another direction, an iceboat turned in narrow circles. Lightning flashed from dark clouds, thunder rolled steadily. Lampley walked to a stairway, iron-railed and steep.

Smell indicated that the floor above was used for chickens. Wire cages reached higher than a man's head, fryers stuck wan beaks through the openings into feed-troughs, pecking in brainless, suicidal intensity: t appetty-tappetty-tappetty tap-tap. Women with arms like thighs and breasts like rumps butchered methodically, wringing necks, cutting throats, chopping heads off. Spattered with blood, the women wiped their eyes with their great forearms, tossing sweaty hair out of their faces, joking, smearing entrails on their filthy aprons. The Governor hastily climbed the shallow wooden stairs ahead.

He was panting a little when he reached the sculptors' studio. Statues towered in impassive marble, porphyry, onyx, granite: men and women, gods and goddesses, dinosaurs, scorpions, dolphins, tortoises, dryads, satyrs, soaring abstractions—multi-planed figures, spheres, subtlety out-of-round, curves and ovals in inescapable relationships. He put his hand against the cold stone; the aloof, remote smoothness reassured him.

Obscured—not hidden, but certainly not put out for all to see—were groups in wood, soapstone, chalk, jade, concrete, glass, bone. Mermaids, centaurs, demons, incubi, basilisks, cockatrices, foetuses, were carved in meticulous detail. Monsters, congenitally malformed, crouched next to cyclops. Multi-limbed children, hermaphrodites, twins joined chest to chest, mouthless, earless, armless creatures. He shuddered away from them, turned back to the nobler creations; always his eye found another collection of horror for him to gaze at.

He was reluctant to leave this place of quietness and aspiration, of fascinating disgust. The stairway leading up was a continuance. The flight was of chalcedony, wide, sweeping upward in the grand manner, curving outward at the base and dividing in two halfway up; it was covered with slime, which bubbled and stank in decay.

He trod fastidiously through the contamination, wiping his feet free of the clinging rot at the top. A bespectacled ape with a stethoscope dangling from the pocket of his white jacket seized Lampley's hand, dug his fingers into the wrist, feeling for the pulse with an unbreakable grip. The jacket was his only garment; it was not quite long enough to cover his genitals.

"Get a stretcher, Nurse," the ape called over his shoulder. He stood on tiptoe to peer first into the Governor's right eye, and then the left, holding the lids open gently.

"There's nothing wrong with me," protested Lampley.

"Let's hope not," murmured the ape soothingly. "We'll soon find out."

Another ape in white cap and starched white skirts pedaled with bare feet a bicycle attached to a gurney. "Just get on this," said the ape-doctor.

"I can walk," contended Lampley.

"We have our rules," insisted the ape-doctor firmly but not unpleasantly. "If you are cooperative it will be easier all around."

The ape-nurse smiled at the Governor, opening her mouth wide to show her fangs. "You can sit, you know; you don't have to lie down."

Lampley seated himself on the edge of the gurney. The ape-nurse pedaled vigorously; the doctor trotted alongside, consulting the bulbous watch on his furry arm. The dial had no hands, numerals or glass, only buttons marked, HOT,

RUTTING, COLD, BANANA, JAVA, RESET. "I don't understand," said Lampley.

"Don't worry," advised the doctor. "None of us understand. Just remember there's nothing to worry about. We're here only to help you."

"But I don't need help."

The two apes exchanged significant glances and the nurse picked a flea off the doctor's thigh. "That's what they all say," commented the doctor pityingly. "It's nothing to be ashamed of. The tempo of uncivilized life is such it's a wonder more don't break under it."

"I—" began the Governor, and stopped. He could deny nothing.

They entered a white-floored room shaped like a teepee, with white walls leaning together, coming to a point at an incandescent light above. The nurse pedaled the gurney under the cone and rested her head on her arms. Five other ape-doctors came through the shining walls, which closed unbroken behind them. "Good-day, Doctor," they greeted in unison.

"Good-day, Doctor," replied the ape-doctor. "We have a most uninteresting case here."

A short ape plucked at his lower lip and grinned at the Governor. "Lucky you," he wheezed in a stage whisper. "He never discharges the interesting ones."

The other apes laughed; even the head doctor had trouble suppressing his smile. "Now, gentle-pithecanthropes," he said, "I'd like to have your opinions."

An emaciated ape with a hearing aid adjusted an ophthalmoscope and squinted at the Governor. "What's its case-history?" he asked gruffly.

"The usual thing: congenital logophilia, the ordinary childhood disorders—inflammation of the gizzard, febrile larynx, minor pyromania, swollen presence—distention of the id, a liberal murmur, optical inversion, pathological increment of the epidermis, cancer of the body politic. Nothing to coruscate a clinician."

"Mmmmm," muttered a muscular ape, balancing himself on his knuckles and shaking his head soberly. "I don't dig these non-arboreal climbers. Smacks of delusion."

"Now Doctor," admonished the head physician, "are you making a diagnosis before all the returns are in? We haven't even started to count the ballots."

"The polls aren't closed yet," the nurse raised her head to point out. "That's a joke, see?"

A fat ape-doctor removed her cap and stuck it on one side of his head. "How's his colostrum?"

"What about his colophon?" inquired an old, stooped, graying ape.

"I'm more interested in his collyrium," said the short ape.

"You're a card, Doctor," cried the fat ape and the muscular ape together.

"Well, well," said the head physician tolerantly. "Fun is fun, but we must consider the patient."

"Consider the patient," ordered the nurse sternly, retrieving her cap.

"Patients are a virtue, get them while you can, hyster in a woman, prostate in a man," chanted the thin ape. "Let's get on with it."

"I see definite signs of softening of the hardening," remarked the old ape.

"Pardon me, Doctor," protested the thin ape, "surely these are classic symptoms of hardening of the softening."

"Weakening of the perspicates," muttered the muscular ape.

"Inversion of the fluctuates," amended the fat ape.

"Disconvection of the interregnum with complicated indications of pronobis-paxvobiscum," said the jovial ape, scratching between his shoulder blades.

"Are we in complete disagreement?" questioned the head doctor cheerfully.

"Apesolutsly, Doctor," confirmed the old consultant. "Apesculapius and Hippocrapes confirm our capabilities."

The nurse whipped a corncob pipe with a long curved stem from under her skirts and stuck it in the fat ape's mouth. The muscular ape rubbed two sticks together till they burst into flame. The thin ape handed over a pair of goggles. When the glasses were adjusted and the pipe going to his satisfaction, the fat ape said, "Let the diagnosis continue. Silence in the court!"

The jovial ape produced a compass and rested it on Lampley's knee. "Shoot the works, cousin," he commanded.

The nurse sang in a growly voice, "The one shines least, the none shines nest, but I know where the run shines in your vest—"

"Silence in the court!" repeated the fat ape. "Spin, cousin."

Lampley looked down at the compass, saw it had no glass. The points were marked, FORTH, Forth Forth-Least, Forth Least by Forth, Forth-Least; Least Forth Least, Forth Least by Least, LEAST; Least by Mouth Least by Least, Mouth Least; Mouth-Mouth-Least, Mouth Least by Mouth, MOUTH; Mouth by Mouth-Best, Mouth-Best by Mouth, Best Mouth, Mouth-Best by Best, Best-Mouth by Best, BEST; Best by Forth-Best, Forth-Best by Best, Forth-Best; Forth-Best by Forth, Forth by Forth-Best, FORTH. The magnetic needle wobbled loosely. Lampley spun it clumsily. The head physician pressed the studs on his watch. All the apes crowded in front of the Governor so he could not see the compass. He knew when the needle stopped, however.

"Incredible!" cried the old ape.

"Beautiful!" cried the fat ape.

"Scientific!" cried the jovial ape.

"On the button!" cried the thin ape.

"Haven't seen anything like it since I was an interne!" cried the muscular ape.

"Very nice," said the head physician. "I take it we are agreed?"

"Unequivocally," said the nurse. "Wow! Let's go!"

"Acute epistomology," said the thin ape tonelessly.

"Chronic voracity," said the fat ape satisfiedly.

"Inflamed igloosensesisty," said the jesting ape happily.

"Dubious proneity," said the old ape solemnly.

"Delusions of humanity," said the muscular ape sadly.

"Delusions of humanity," repeated the whole college mournfully.

"Good, very good indeed," observed the head physician, swinging from a trapeze and playing a xylophone with his toes. "Hold him temporarily under observation—"

"No sedation, Doctor," warned the old ape.

"No medication, Doctor," enjoined the muscular ape.

"No inflation, Doctor," suggested the thin ape.

"No castration, Doctor," put in the jovial ape.

"No vindication, Doctor," added the fat ape.

"—pending release and discharge," concluded the head doctor.

"What about infection?" asked the nurse.

"Humanity is not contagious," they all reminded her together.

The practitioners took pomegranates, figs, dates, mangoes and papayas from their jacket pockets and began munching them earnestly. The nurse pedaled Lampley through the white walls. "Are you ever lucky," she informed him chattily. "They might have put you in a straitjacket and fed you orally."

"But there's nothing wrong with me."

"Get tired," advised the nurse. "Your needle is stuck." She dismounted. "Stay where you are," she said when he started to get off too. "So long, cousin—don't take any wooden colonies."

The gurney moved on by itself, picking up speed. It careened through dazzling corridors, down ramps, up inclines, through wards, at such a dizzying pace he could see only the footrails of the beds with their clipboards of charts. Doors flipped open at his coming and swung back after him. Finally the gurney stopped so suddenly he slid forward smoothly onto the floor. When he picked himself up the vehicle was whizzing around a corner.

He was on a turntable, so nicely fitted into the floor that only a hairline crack defined it. It revolved slowly past curious scenes of men and women being cupped and leeched, poulticed with manure or steaming tripes, packed in snow, offered acrid inhalants or foul broths; of madmen worshipped or chained and beaten, of babies deformed for beauty's sake and old people eaten for economy's.

When he stepped off the turntable he was in a pleasant but definitely institutionalized room. An elderly man, derby hatted, blew patiently into a mute saxophone. A woman with waist-long white hair, lips drawn in sharply over empty gums, passed an unthreaded shuttle across a loom. A girl, rocking evenly back and forth, smiled knowingly, secretively. A bald man with dirty cheeks and smudged scalp, his tongue caught intently between his teeth, lay prone before a collection of posters, carefully painting mustaches on the faces of women, blotting out the faces of men.

At the other end of the room the Governor saw his mother. She was knitting slowly, diligently. Her arthritis, he thought sympathetically. He went to her. "Hello Mother." He kissed her cheek.

She finished two more stitches before she spoke. "How are you, Almon?" she asked placidly. "Isn't this a charming place?"

"You like it here, Mother?"

"Well, it isn't like being in one's own home. And of course they do serve lamb chops without the paper frills," she complained. "I suppose it's all right, but I must say they look rather naked."

"But you're all right otherwise ?"

"My eyes bother me, there's something wrong with the lights. The food hurts my gums and I'm short of breath and I never can seem to get comfortable clothes that aren't dowdy. And the newspapers are full of horrors—"

"Yes, yes," he interrupted impatiently. "But they treat you well, don't they?"

She put down her knitting. "It depends entirely what you mean by that, Almon. If your poor father had lived no one would ever have hustled me around the way they do here."

"Are they rude to you, Mother?"

"They certainly don't act as I should expect persons to act toward a lady."

"They don't—they don't handle you roughly?"

"My dear boy! What a question. They wouldn't dare."

He sank into a chair. "That's good. It's all right then."

"I shouldn't go as far as to say that." She resumed her knitting. "They read my letters," she announced in a loud whisper.

"What letters?" he asked.

"Now Almon, don't pry."

"I'm sorry, Mother. I only thought there might be something I could do about it."

"Don't be ridiculous, Almon. What could a boy do about such things?"

He was silent, despondent. "Oh, Mother…" He wanted to say that it was too easy to dismiss all questions as having too many answers or none at all—to say that the simplest questions, the ones apparently most irrelevant or meaningless were least susceptible of reply. What he wanted to say was true enough—or rather, it was true, but not enough. There were no answers, yet everything was an answer of sorts. "Oh, Mother," he said, "I don't know."

"Of course you don't," she agreed sharply. "Here, wind my wool for me."

Obediently he picked up the strand lying on her lap and began looping it around her outstretched hands. The yarn was kinked and lusterless. "Where do you get your wool?" he asked conversationally.

She cackled. "Now dear boy, don't try to catch me on one as old as that. I simply will not say from the sheep I count when I'm going to sleep. I just won't."

"I'm sorry, Mother."

"Are you really? Truly contrite? Genuinely humble?"

"I—I suppose so."

"Oh, suppositions. Theories. Vapors. Hopes. Pooh. Gracious, can't you wind faster?"

"Something seems to be holding the wool back."

"Nonsense! Oh, see what you've done, you clumsy boy! You're unraveling my cushion."

"I'm sorry, Mother."

She hurled her knitting in his face. "Take him away," she screamed. "He's a monster—can't you see?"

The other inmates threw up their heads and howled in unison. One sufferer, naked to the waist, his distorted face set in a dreadful smile, his hands stiffened into claws, ran into the room and danced around the Governor. Two women, their streaming hair starched with dirt, shrieked, "He did it, he did it. He's the peeping tom." A man shambled in a circle, head down, muttering, "Womb, tomb, boom; boom, womb, tomb; tomb, boom, womb."

Two sternly expressionless attendants led the Governor to the elevator. "You are discharged for conduct unbecoming a patient and a gentle."

"But I—"

"If it weren't for this," said one of the attendants coldly, indicating his white coat, "I'd call you out myself, you cad."

"Don't demean yourself, brother," urged the other attendant. "He'll suffer now."

A group of orderlies appeared. Those in front beat upon enamel sputum dishes with hammers used to test reflexes. After them came a number with dilators, tubes and other objects, which they employed as fifes and flutes. The color-bearer dipped his caduceus to the ground while the band played the rogues' march. A doctor drew his scalpel and cut the Governor's buttons from the cuff of his jacket.

The elevator doors opened. The clerk peeled off a white smock and tossed it out. "Step to the rear of the car please," he urged the Governor.

Lampley stumbled in. The elevator swished upward, then ran backward for interminable miles. It stopped; mechanics with rubber wrenches, paper hammers and cloth screwdrivers removed the steel doors, replacing them with a glass one. The clerk moved the control lever; the elevator rose again.

Once more it was in the shaft lined with porcelain-faced bricks. The Governor noticed how meticulously they had been set in place, each fitting so neatly against the next, no course of mortar thicker than the one above or below.

The clerk left the door open and leaned against it as Lampley wandered between the rows of grand pianos. The drops from the stalactites tinkled as monotonously as before on the exposed strings of the instruments. Plink plink, plink plink, plink plunk. It seemed to him—he was by no means sure—that on his first visit the pianos had all been identical. Now they were rosewood, mahogany, maple, ebony. Some were enameled a startling white, one gleamed in dull silver, the varnish on another sparkled with crushed glass. He paused before a grand of such modest finish and unobtrusive wood that it commanded instant attention among more flamboyant peers. The Governor sat down before it, striking a key with his middle finger. Plink. What a work is man, he thought; I will my finger to move and it moves—what incomparable engineering! Plink. He had forgotten even how to play a scale; the stalactites could do as well or better. Plink plink, plink plunk.

In imagination he played the piano with perfect mastery, without effort, without barrier between conception and performance. The exquisite music flowed from his fingers and laved the air. His heart burst with exaltation. The power of his playing infected all the nearby pianos; they exploded into the same melody.

Plink plink. Miss Brewster would have said primly, "If that was your ambition, you should have practiced." Hours and hours and hours every day. Plink plink. And then Miss Brewster would not have smacked his hands and when he thought of her when he was bigger he wouldn't have... Plink plunk. A stupid fancy.

He got up impatiently. Could that be the unicorn lurking in the shadows? He walked slowly toward it. The creature showed no fear of him, made no attempt to run away.

Trembling a little, Lampley put out his hand. The unicorn nuzzled his palm. Lampley touched the golden horn, ran his fingers through the foamy mane. The unicorn looked at him with its blue eyes; Lampley felt infinitely rewarded.

The unicorn was smaller than he had thought—as small as a pony. They walked together between the pianos, the beast breathing gently, the man reassuring himself of affection by rubbing the soft coat. All the pain of struggle began slowly to drain from his body; he knew he could be content to stay here.

Only when they were almost at the elevator did the unicorn throw up his head, toss his mane and gallop off. The Governor turned to pursue but the clerk, still leaning in the open door, stopped him. "It's no use," he called, not unkindly. "You couldn't catch him unless he wanted you to."

"But he..." began Lampley.

"A whim," said the clerk. "They're all alike."

Sadly he entered the elevator. It was only as the door was closing he realized the plinking from the stalactites had stopped as he touched the unicorn.

CHAPTER EIGHT

THE elevator slid upward steadily through the white-tiled shaft. Lampley, slowly recovering his calm after the loss of the unicorn, caught glimpses of the activities in the various sub-basements. Men were building a ship in one, laying the keel, riveting the ribs, welding the plates. Higher, dynamos of all sizes were attended by midgets who climbed and clung like flies. On the next floor hundreds of seamstresses in Grecian robes cut and sewed balloons, twisted silk threads into heavy ropes, wove rush baskets and attached them to the flaccid bags; on another he saw a congregation of worshippers at prayer. There was a sub-basement that was a library, one which was a toy factory, one where alchemists turned waste into gold. There was a bakery, an automobile assembly, an iron foundry, a chemical laboratory, a college, a mortuary. They rose through moving picture stages, distilleries, warehouses, millwrights, armorers, perfume makers, silversmiths, glass-blowers, gem-cutters, machine-shops, art galleries, a mint, lumberyard, stoveworks.

Then came a series of vacant floors: bleak, void, stale. The elevator moved much more slowly now, as though dragged down by the emptiness, pulled back, hampered by the blankness through which it was passing.

"About this fellow," said the clerk abruptly.

"What fellow?" parried the Governor. But he knew.

The clerk pulled out a plastic mask and slipped it over his face. It was a replica of his own features, subtly altered, so that the Governor was filled with sick terror at the sight of mouth, nose, cheeks, eyes, superimposed on those which differed only enough to be totally alien. The clerk stopped the elevator, opened the door. Walls of rough stone towered on all sides. The Governor held back until the clerk's steady stare forced him out onto the cracked. uneven pavement. There was a sweetish, sickening, vaguely familiar smell all around.

The clerk rubbed his hands together and then over Lampley's arm in a gesture of appraisal and possession. To his disgust the Governor saw the fabric of his jacket crumble and dissolve. His jacket and the shirt beneath, leaving his skin and flesh bare and vulnerable. The touch of the fingers was loathsome but he was unable to draw away from it. The clerk brought his face close, so that Lampley saw where the mouth of the mask, the eyeholes and nostrils failed to match those beneath.

"This man, this convict, this felon. You couldn't find it in you to reprieve him?"

"He had a fair trial," mumbled Lampley.

"A fair trial," repeated the clerk. "The jurors were gods, the judge was justice incarnate?"

"The judge was properly assigned; the jurors were members of a qualified panel."

"Your prerogative...?"

"My prerogative is to temper justice with mercy."

"And you were unable?"

"He murdered his father. He strangled him, he smothered him with a pillow, he stabbed him in the heart, he poisoned him, he shot him with a pistol; he killed his mother."

"Are you sure?" asked the clerk, puffing out the cheeks of his mask.

"There were witnesses, there was circumstantial evidence, he confessed. He clubbed his mother to death, he cut her throat, he held her under water till she died."

"Ah," sighed the clerk. "Ah... Then no reprieve was possible?"

"No reprieve was possible," replied the Governor firmly.

"So be it," said the clerk.

Two pale men leapt from their hiding-place and bound Lampley's hands behind him. They led him through an archway into a courtyard. A masked executioner came forward and knelt at his feet. "I ask your forgiveness, noble sir, for what I am about. The deed is not mine, I am but a servitor."

The two pressed him toward the block and forced his head low. The semicircular hollow was cunningly contrived to fit any neck. The long gashes in the wood pulled and sucked at his throat. The executioner raised his ax and brought it down. Lampley's head rolled in the sawdust beyond the scaffold.

The two seized him and bound his arms. From a distance he heard the chaplain's breaking voice. They hustled him between the stone walls and dragged him up the gallows' steps. The hood was dropped over his head, then the rope. He felt the hardness of the knot against his left ear. There was no spittle in his mouth. They pushed his legs firmly into place over the trap. He heard the snick of the knife as it cut the cords. He swung in a narrowing circle.

They wrapped the thin cord deftly round and round his body, pinioning his arms cruelly to his sides. They slid him down the incline beneath the guillotine. When he was suitably in place the blade descended swiftly.

They seated him in the chair and strapped the electrodes to his leg and head. They pushed him into the sealed chamber and watched through greedy slits while the cyanide pellets were released. They tied the bandage over his eyes and stepped back just before the fusillade.

He lay broken on the rough stones. He remembered the touch of the golden horn and began breathing again. He remembered the island under the earth and his heart resumed beating. He remembered the young girl in the hotel and he could see and hear.

He rose slowly and viewed his bodies after their agonies. He walked past the bullet-chipped wall, the gas chamber, electric chair, guillotine, gallows. His feet scuffed the bloody sawdust by the headsman's block.

The elevator stood empty and unattended. He went into the car, the door closed behind him and the car shot up. Again it slowed as it passed the darkened tiles in the upper reaches of the sub-basements, so that it was once more moving sluggishly as the lobby and the hall above came in sight. It stopped amid the elegance of the third floor, and the doors opened of themselves.

The elegance had become shabby beyond restoration. The thick carpet was worn to the threads. Woodwork and paneling no longer contrasted, they were the same uniform color of age. The chairs and sofas were ripped and tattered, their stuffing protruded like ruptures. The doll was in the same place and position; a pendulous belly and two elongated breasts had been sewed on with coarse stitches.

The iron railing around the quadrangle leaned outward; some of the balusters were missing. The concourse below was gone; he looked down on the dingy lobby, past the visible portion of the second floor hiding the reception desk. He turned away; the doors, which had borne the esoteric numerals, were blank, their panels warped and sagging.

He searched for the wide staircase to the second floor. His orientation had changed, he turned left instead of right, or right instead of left. In lieu of the grand flight he came upon a mean descent, twisting every few steps. The boards creaked and quivered under his weight.

His room was that of the first door he opened. His handbag rested on the foot of the bed, the wax figures of the bride and groom stood stiffly in the cloudy glass bell. Lampley tarried before the mirror, adjusting his sleeves, assuring himself there was neither lint nor soil on his jacket. He picked up his bag and gave a conventional last glance around, though he knew he had brought nothing more into the room.

He shut the door and tried the handle; it did not turn. Yet surely it had been closed before he went in to retrieve his bag? All the doors on the hall were shut, shut and locked and untenanted, their invitation withdrawn. He reached the narrow stairs. From these there was no landing halfway down, nor did they lead to the lobby. They ended at a solid door with a handle instead of a knob. He pressed the latch down doubtfully, anxious to be out of this blind end, unwilling to go back up and start down again.

The refrigerator room, which had been so cold, was now warm and stuffy. There was no igloo. The game and fish were gone, the brine barrels were tipped over, gaping unconcernedly. They gave out no smell save that of old wood. The sawdust had weathered. Most of the meat hooks were empty; from a few hung the bare skeletons of beeves and sheep and swine, the surface of their bones dry, cracked with long, thin crevices, crossed with fine hairlines. He recognized the buffalo because of the peculiar shape of the skull and horns lying on the floor below the carcass.

He pushed open the massive door to the kitchen. The old man was carving a set of chessmen out of bone; several finished pieces, rooks, knights and a queen stood in a row before him. In his thick fingers the other queen was taking recognizable shape. All had the same distortion as the plaster figures in the wall. He looked up at Lampley without interrupting his work. "A hard time, hay?"

The Governor nodded. The old man jerked a thumb over his shoulder. Lampley followed its direction into the eating room. The idiot was trying to spoon soup into his mouth, spilling most of it, sputtering the rest into slimy bubbles. The clerk, his eyes closed, had one leg hooked over the corner of the table. The woman smiled at him, showing the gold tooth. There was no sign of the girl. Lampley sat down in the old man's place.

The clerk's eyes opened; the mask was gone. He pushed a hard crust of bread across the table. Lampley picked it up and turned it over in his fingers. "I'm going," he announced to them.

The clerk yawned. "I'd be afraid myself," he confessed.

"Afraid of what?" asked the Governor.

The clerk shrugged. "So much," he said hazily. "Everything." He smiled doubtfully.

"There's nothing to be afraid of," said the Governor boldly.

The clerk shook his head and left the room. The idiot gurgled and sputtered over his soup. Lampley reached for the corner of the napkin tied around his neck and wiped the drooling mouth. He took the stale crust and broke it into the soup. When the bits were soaked he used the spoon to feed them slowly to his son.

"It's no use," said the woman. "You can't teach him."

"I wasn't trying—" began Lampley, and let it go. "Where is your sister?"

She wrinkled her forehead. "Sister?"

He had asked the girl if she were this woman's daughter; she is my sister, she had said, and then something horrible— what?—happened. He could not be mistaken. "The girl who was here."

"I was the only girl here. There was no other. There never was another."

He looked at her searchingly; her face showed no disingenuousness. He finished feeding the defective and wiped his face again. He got up and went over to the woman. She reached out her hand to touch his. He bent and kissed her. Then he kissed his son.

In the lobby the clerk was behind the desk, idly searching through the empty pigeonholes. "Nothing for you," he said without turning around.

The Governor went through the entrance and down the steps into the afternoon sunlight. When he came to his car he reached in his pocket for the keys. His hand touched his watch. He pulled it out and saw it was running, the sweep second hand revolving inexorably. He slipped it on his wrist and unlocked the car door.

Before getting in he glanced up and down the street and back at the hotel. He had never seen it or the town at any time in his life.

THE END

A SUDDEN BREAK IN THE STREAM OF TIME

Les Ackerman was in his lab experimenting with a new element. Suddenly there was the blinding flash of a nuclear explosion that blew nearly everything around him— seemingly—sky-high! But while some things appeared to have been completely destroyed, others seemed perfectly intact— including Les Ackerman himself! However, Ackerman discovered quickly that something was terribly wrong. While he could see and hear everything around him, he could only physically touch a limited number of things. His arms and hands waved wildly through walls and doors as though he was a phantom entity. And unfortunately for Les, no one could see or hear him—or so it seemed for a while. For Ackerman would soon find himself sought-after by the denizens of three possible worlds, all contending that only he could correct the incredible situation that faced mankind. The only problem was that Les Ackerman didn't know what he'd done!

CAST OF CHARACTERS

LES ACKERMAN
This research physicist meddled with a new element and set off a chain of events that shook the universe to its foundation.

TANSIE LEE
She was seemingly from another reality—and she appeared to love Les Ackerman for reasons he wasn't quite sure of.

CALVIN BLAINE
Another person from another reality. He wanted Ackerman to "fix" the problem he had created—before it was too late.

LAURIE BLAINE
Innocent, sweet, and effervescent—but were her motives as pure and innocent as they seemed?

BARRY FORD
Yet another person from a different "time-space." His mission was to get Les Ackerman to help save the Earth—or Earths!

JOAN LAPLANE
An eye-catching brunette—good at facts and figures—who promised not to use her beauty to sway Ackerman.

THE
WORLD-MOVER

By
GEORGE O. SMITH

ARMCHAIR FICTION
PO Box 4369, Medford, Oregon 97501-0168

*For more information about Armchair Books and products, visit our
website at…*

www.armchairfiction.com

Or email us at…

armchairfiction@yahoo.com

CHAPTER ONE

TO THE present sitting, there were three hundred thousand words in the report on the new transuranic element that Les Ackerman was studying. This took months of painstaking work, but Ackerman viewed his results with satisfaction. To date, the report covered about all that was to be known regarding the physical and chemical properties of this new element; there remained only the nuclear properties to investigate.

Nuclear properties were always left to last. Nuclear bombardment defiled the element and rendered it unsuitable for the undestructive chemical analysis and physical investigations.

So Les Ackerman closed his notebook with a slam and checked the refrigerator. The deuterium-ice—frozen heavy water—for the cyclotron target was in fine shape. He could start at once.

He took both the ice-target and the sample to the big, enclosed room and inserted them in the proper places in the cyclotron set-up. Then he fired up the big cyclotron, and high-energy deuterons bombarded the deuterium-ice target, releasing free neutrons that in turn bombarded the sample.

That was to be his last job for the night; the registering counters would record the radioactivity while he slept, and in the morning the sample would probably be "cold" enough to handle. He consulted his prospectus in the notebook and checked the bombardment-time for this first nuclear test. One half-hour. At the end of one half-hour, Ackerman could turn off the cyc and go to bed. The automatic counters would quietly record the diminishing activity of the "hot" sample.

The click of the counting-rate meter sounded. The first atoms of the sample were being attacked properly. Ackerman nodded to himself, there in the operating chamber, separated from the real activity by solid yards of concrete, water, and paraffin.

Unluckily, Ackerman could not be in the eye chamber itself to watch. As it was, it would have been no more dangerous for Les to stand in the radioactivity-laden cyclotron room than it was for him here in what all cyclotron mechanics considered more than safe from harm.

As the neutrons raced invisibly into the new element, a tiny, glistening sphere expanded, millimeter by millimeter. It was a strange field of energy, a true freak of Nature. Unpredicted and unknown, it hovered at nine centimeters radius as the sample swallowed neutrons by the uncounted million. It expanded again, slowly, slowly, slowly until the critical proportion of sample and transmuted nuclei was attained.

Then the glistening sphere of energy expanded with an acceleration that drove it to the ends of the infinite universe in a matter of microseconds. Too swift to be seen, to register—if there had been a means of detecting it—and too swift even to leave a trace of evidence on the physical universe.

ITS EFFECT, however, was evident to Ackerman. The others who came later saw only what they found remaining. Les was on the spot, and saw the dual effect of the bombardment of Element X by neutrons.

His notebook gave the first sight of unreality. Like a double exposure, or a photomontage, he saw page after page curl up in charred destruction—curling up wraithlike out of a complete and unharmed volume! He saw the solid concrete blocks rave into incandescence—flying in terrible fury out of the unharmed wall; each brick as it exploded separating ghost-like from its unharmed twin. The laboratory exploded in a mighty pillar of flame and fire—rising seventy thousand feet into the sky but mushrooming upward from the placidly unharmed ghostly replica of itself. The light from the explosion was all blinding, yet the calm moonlight still cast its mellow shadow over the unharmed buildings. The explosion shocked fleecy clouds into falling rain—rain that fell from the serenely existing sky of the other—other—other what?

Ackerman found himself standing on the sterile land that surrounded the laboratory, simultaneously watching the boiling cloud above and the moonlit laboratory below. He was puzzled, somewhat afraid to go close to the possible effect of the nuclear explosion; yet there was the fact that at least in one existence the laboratory was unharmed.

He waited, wondering. The passage of time did not seem to bother him. Previously, Ackerman had been tired, and more than glad that this was the last job of the evening. Now he was far from weary, and the passage of time was difficult to estimate.

He was surprised to see, not too much later, that people were streaming towards the scene. He laughed at one group—a racing column of excellent fire-fighting equipment; the idea of tossing water or chemicals on a radioactive explosion was amusing in a sense. The fire had gone out a microsecond or so after it had started, and if anything were burning now, it was because the stuff had not time to cool down yet. Ackerman could think of nothing more dangerous, however, than to drive a fire truck—or anything else not shielded in lead, water, and concrete—across the scorched area.

He saw his colleagues walking wraithlike and arguing heatedly against the police and firemen. The latter wanted to go in; Ackerman's former mates were waving counters and personal ionization meters at them, trying to explain the danger. The officials were inclined to be skeptical of any danger that could not be seen, but were equally awed by the names of the men who barred their way. At long last a crude circle was drawn on the ground; as the curious folk continued to arrive, the circle was quickly filled and people were standing with their toes across the line.

ACKERMAN found one of his friends near him. "Crowley!" he called.

Tom Crowley did not hear; he continued to argue with another fellow about Ackerman.

"No," said Ackerman. "I'm here—not up in that cloud!"

"Poor Les," said Tom. "I wonder what happened."

Ed Waters shrugged sorrowfully. "I can't imagine; there was certainly nothing dangerous in what Les was intending to do."

"And we know Les," replied Tom. "He'd not take to doing something off the beam."

"There was certainly nothing off the beam about bombarding Element X with neutrons," agreed Ed Waters. "We've done it before."

"But not with as large a sample. We'll have to be careful in the future about it."

Waters grinned wolfishly. "We'll not toss another cyclotron to the breeze," he said. "We can get a neutron-emitting radioisotope from one of the uranium piles and shove the two together by remote control; it'll save both lives and materiel."

"Too damned bad," said Crowley. "We lost a good man."

"But I'm right here!" exploded Ackerman. He had been standing between them, waving his hands in their faces—and in more than one case *through* their faces. Strangely enough, the trees and the ground were quite solid to Les Ackerman, but his friends were not.

The crowds of the curious came and they went; newspapers, as the hours went on, told Ackerman that he was the victim of a terrible atomic blast, a totally deplorable situation.

Ackerman wondered more about it. Was this death?

*　*　*

IT WAS MANY hours later, when daylight had come fully and the morning's work was to begin, that Les Ackerman got his next shock. The sterile area was still guarded by Ackerman's friends, making close watch with counters and ionization meters. Yet so far as Les was concerned, the shallow depression of greenish glaze fell in a concave bowl below the surface of a serene and untouched terrain upon which the wraithlike laboratory stood. He termed it "wraithlike" because he could see both the greenish depression and the laboratory, and the other side of the blast-bowl through the laboratory. He could not see through the laboratory to glimpse any of its insides.

Whatever this division was, Ackerman could see a dual possibility, could see either the world of the explosion or he could see the world of peace and quiet.

His shock came as the technicians began to arrive. Then, he blinked. As he was standing beside Ed Waters, he saw Waters' car drive up to the parking place beside the laboratory, saw Ed emerge and enter the building by the main door!

Before he could follow Waters, he saw Tom Crowley enter, too; Ackerman left their counterparts on the edge of the seared area and raced forward with a shout of alarm.

It occurred to him, then, that both men carried personal counters and warning gauges; they would have been warned away from the area if there were any radioactive danger. Ackerman found his hand passing through the door-handle and puzzled over how to get in until he understood that if his hand could pass through the door handle, he himself might pass through the door. He did, and with some dismay knew that he was walking, not upon the floor of the building but about a foot or so below the floor. With an effort of his will alone Les raised himself; it was disconcerting to know that he was wading knee deep through a solid concrete floor.

He found Waters and Crowley in the cyclotron room. They were looking over the sample critically with heavy magnifiers and making notes. "Thought Les was going to flop here," said Waters.

"So did I. He must have decided to go home after he was finished."

"Don't blame him. I'd have been inclined to set the timers and leave then. "Ackerman is a cautious fellow and would wait until the timers clicked off even though he had nothing to do but sit and watch unerring meters. I'd say that Les deserved a good night's sleep. Well, take a hunk off of the sample for the radio-isotopists, and we'll carve a bit ourselves for later, then give the remaining piece another banging."

"You carve," said Crowley. "I'll get another heavy-ice target from the refrigerator."

Waters nodded, cut two infinitesimal slices from the sample with a diamond-edged wheel, dropped them into separate containers and labeled them both. Then he re-inserted the sample in the cyclotron set-up and both men went out to give the Element X sample a second shot—according to plan, a longer and more energetic blast.

Vainly Les Ackerman tried to reach them.

He screamed himself hoarse, trying to tell them not to do it—that he had been a one-time victim. Then, in fear and desperation, he saw them leave the cyclotron chamber; he fought and swore against his wraithlike fingers that passed through the sample of death. He clawed ineffectively at it, trying to take it from the coming blast of neutrons. Like the room, the walls, and the men, his hands passed through the cyclotron; through the sample; and through the containing shell. Instinctively he knew that the cyclotron was being fired up, yet his fumbling hand's felt nothing of the fifty thousand volt driving power of the Dee plates. He knew instinctively when the storm of the deuterons came to bombard the heavy-water ice he knew that the resulting neutrons were entering the sample of Element X.

He fumed and fretted; then as his mind cried out in vain, his will slipped and Les Ackerman went down through the floor of the room, he could not reach up high enough even to touch the imminent danger.

He turned and ran, almost crying in frustration.

Near the seared edge of last night's explosion, Ackerman turned to watch. An hour passed—Two—Three.

Whatever had happened before, it was not to happen again. Not this time, at least.

For when Les returned, Waters and Crowley were watching the brief half-lives die out on the counters and making histograms in an effort to predict the safety-time.

*   *   *

Mystified, tired of wondering, and utterly lonesome, Les Ackerman waited in the no-world life between two direct possibilities of man's existence.

It was meaningless to Ackerman; perhaps it was meaningless to Nature herself.

The complete incongruity of it all—and the conflicting evidences were beyond him. Trees and rock and ground were one; the building was there and so was that sere bowl of greenish glaze. At nightfall, his friends entered their cars by the laboratory and drove right through the still-crowding people of the other existence. Waters passed almost through his alter ego, and might have seen his friend Crowley twice—excepting that Waters, unlike Les Ackerman, could not see both coincident pathways of event.

CHAPTER TWO

WEARY, utterly lonesome, and completely baffled about it all, Les Ackerman finally slept. On the hard ground he slept, loath to leave the scene.

He was awakened by the sound of a voice speaking his name. Shaking his head, Les sat up, saw that it was just about sunrise, and answered instinctively, though he knew that his voice could not be heard. He could hear people—but people could not hear him; just as he could see people but they could not see him.

"I'm right here," he said for, perhaps, the ten-thousandth time. He expected, for the ten-thousandth time, that he would not be heard.

"Good," replied the voice.

Then in the growing light, Ackerman saw a glistening, egg-shaped vehicle coming slowly through the grove of trees. It hovered above him and settled easily to the ground.

The voice, he saw, came from a woman who was obviously driving the thing. There was a small hemisphere of glass thrown back from the "top" of the vehicle, and the woman was head and shoulders above the level of the hull.

She smiled, and Ackerman was instantly attracted. "Well," she said with an air of successful finality. "You've arrived."

Ackerman shrugged. So far as he was concerned, the girl could get out of the vehicle and make passes at him; he was still as isolated from all people as a butterfly in a glass case at some moldy museum.

"Have I?" he answered, still skeptical.

"You have." She ducked her head down into the vehicle and reappeared, coming out of a door in the side. He was a little surprised at her clothing. He expected something bizarre—at least she might have been dressed in something in keeping with the completely exotic vehicle she was driving.

But she was dressed in a simple frock of silk or nylon. Tasteful, modern. She was auburn-haired and very attractive according to Les Ackerman's fastidious standards.

"I'm Tansie Lee," she said, offering a slender hand. He took it and found it firm and warm.

"I'm Les Ack—"

"I know; after all, I've come a long way to find you."

"Me?" asked Ackerman in complete wonder.

"You don't really know what happened?" Her tone was teasing, and she was obviously enjoying every moment of it.

"No, not really," he said. "All I know is that I was bombarding Element X with neutrons and then—well, it's rather hard to describe I can lean against a tree, but I can also walk through the laboratory door. That doesn't make sense."

"Yes it does when you're properly introduced to your environment. Look, Les, you are in the middle, lost territory between two branching streams of events. In one branch, you were the victim of an explosion; in the other, your efforts were successful in the lab.

"Now," she said, groping for the right words so that her explanation would be simple, "a tree might be in both worlds; therefore you can lean against it. If a woodcutter in one branch of events cuts the tree down, then you could walk through it in the other branch. The laboratory is there in one branch only; the green bowl of atomic explosion is there in the other. Follow?"

Ackerman let that digest for a moment and then said: "What would happen if I tried to break off a tree branch myself?"

She laughed. "You'd find—and you'll find—that things consist only of Aristotelian extremes. Either they are non-coincident and therefore very intangible, or you'll find that they are coincident and as untouchable as tungsten carbide to the bare hands. You can walk through non-coincident granite but you couldn't make a dent in coincident tissue paper."

"Then how do my life processes continue? Either I must be breathing coincident—and therefore untouchable and unchangeable air—or I must be breathing non-coincident and therefore untouchable and unchangeable air."

She laughed heartily. "Trouble is, Les Ackerman, you don't really exist; therefore your life processes are unreal."

"Oh—I don't exist, hey? Then what is this that is I?"

"I'll skip the metaphysics," she said with a laugh. "Do you doubt the reality of unreal things?"

"Isn't that a disclaimer in itself?"

SHE SHOOK her head. "The square root of minus one is an unreal number. It is a pure formulation, and yet it is an important factor. You cannot dig too deeply into any phase of science without using it—and yet it is still an imaginary quantity. It does not truly exist, nor do you. Yet it is there as a formulation, and that is what you and I should add: I—are, or am, or whichever."

He laughed too, at her confusion. "We are," he said, but it was more of a question that a correction of her grammar.

"We are—and there are and will be others, too."

"But I do not understand it at all."

"It is not to be easily understood," said Tansie. "Not without help. I'll help, if you want."

"I'd be happy to know what the answer is," said Les. "Just how do you propose to help?"

"My machine. Take a ride?"

He nodded. "I'm hungry; have you any groceries in that thing?"

"While we're following the world line," she promised, "I'll show you that I can cook, too. Come on!"

Tansie led him cheerfully into the vehicle and closed the top-hatch. "We'll be heading into space," she said in a matter-of-fact tone.

"Space?" he gurgled.

She nodded.

"But *why?*"

"In our—condition—being sort of trapped between two world lines, we are swept along in synchronism with the 'temporal advance' of the massive Earth. The Earth is moving through 'space'. Since we have little free 'temporal inertia', we are instantly drawn to whatever era lies in the physical mass. Follow?"

"Not too well, but it sounds like saying that if the four o'clock train arrives now, it must be four o'clock."

Tansie laughed. "We go to the 'space' where Earth will be in a hundred years. Then, having no 'temporal inertia', we are drawn through time to that 'instant'... You know as well as I do that our language of words and subject-predicate sentences dissects events into artificially blocked-off units like 'time' and 'space'. But these inadequate bits of word-magic make you feel better... People not trapped in 'free time' are possessed of almost infinite 'temporal inertia' and the natural gravitational attraction between masses in the main activating force."

Ackerman nodded. "I suppose that indicates some sort of intrinsic motion?"

"Not necessarily."

"But all things are relative."

Tansie thought for a moment. "I don't understand."

"If all things are relative, then position must be."

Tansie looked blank. "I'm asking no questions," she said. "But 'time', too, must be relative. And I know that 'time' is relative to 'space', too. The entropy factors change near massive bodies. Why not 'time?' 'Time' changes with velocity, as does mass. 'Time', mass, and velocity are all factors."

"You forgot energy. Velocity is a function of energy, which is interchangeable with mass, which affects the 'temporal strains'. The whole is one—or in less elision, they are all manifestations of one another."

Tansie smiled, stood up from the control of the ship, and beckoned with her thumb. "You're the brilliant physicist," she said. "But I'll bet I can fry a non-existent egg better than you can."

"Mind if I ask where you get these imaginary eggs?"

The girl laughed and tossed her auburn hair at him. "Real hens lay real eggs. There are two possibilities—"

"I know," he said, joining in with her good spirits. "Either we have a gang of 'time-trapped' poultry, or the art of getting 'time-trapped' along with an icebox full of provender—takes a firm stand somewhere along the line."

"There's means," she admitted.

"Okay," he said. "You cook—and also explain to me just why you seem to think I'm the brilliant one."

"We know you are," she said; "you bear the necessary knowledge to avert disaster."

"Me?"

"You." She pointed at him with a flapjack-flipper, then used it to fracture the shell of an egg. "But no explanation of that right now; it's too gosh-darned complicated. Wait until you learn more about it, and it'll save us all a lot of time."

"But I'm curious."

"Naturally," she said with a whimsical smile. "But I'm going to make the best of this trip, and I don't want to spend every waking hour in explanation; you'd grow tired of me."

THE SMELL of bacon and eggs permeated the place. Les lifted his face and made a show of flaring nostrils sniffing hungrily. The aroma of toast was added, to which was again the odor of butter hitting the hot toast.

"If that tastes as well as it sounds to the nose," he grinned, "I could take a lot of your company."

Tansie whirled the plate before him, placed a cup of coffee beside it. Then she sat across the table from him with her own plate and plied her knife and fork in silence.

He wondered about Tansie; she was singularly receptive to his likes and dislikes, even to the idea of not talking while he was eating. He said nothing until the coffee, and then he looked up and smiled. "That," he said, "was to the taste of Caesar."

She dropped a curtsy that was not well executed because she was not wearing the kind of skirt that makes a curtsy the sweeping genuflection it was intended for. "I render unto Caesar that which is Caesar's."

What stuck foremost in his mind was the fact that Tansie had neglected to supply sugar and cream for the coffee—which might have been a natural gesture—and he wondered whether she knew that he used neither. He did not press the question; he would let more evidence pile up before he accused her of being able to read his mind.

"You'll be interested in a look outside," she said.

"Why?"

"We're not many months ahead, so far. The trees have fallen, and greened again; yet there is sufficient non-coincident growth to make the sight somewhat bizarre."

They went to the control cabin and Tansie slowed the ship until the gray haze outside diminished and the landscape became clear again. The sight was strange. Now, instead of coincident trees, only the main branches were single. The leaves were in that "temporal" double exposure, since the twin worlds were beginning to lose their twinship, each following its own line of future.

"Weird," he agreed, "but I thought we'd be heading into 'space' for certain."

"We are in 'space'," she said. "So far as true 'time' is concerned. The earth is way back there." She pointed off vaguely in a gesture that embraced a full fifty degrees. "Trouble is that this heap wouldn't space-hop worth a tin cent in real life. But remember, we have little true inertia, and therefore a bit of propulsion does a lot of work against a minute mass. It also is less a matter of protection than convenience. You could get out now if you wanted to."

"No," he said.

"But we will stop to stretch our legs after lunch." That, too, struck Les Ackerman in the right pocket.

TANSIE HAD picked him up at about six o'clock in the morning, and the time between then and the clock's registration of noon was pleasant. The girl was brightly amusing and bafflingly vague as it pleased her fancy. She intrigued Ackerman's interest dearly, and the liking was heightened by the almost certain fact that she knew much more about the thing, but was not telling. There was time, she said. Most of the talk was light, or deliberately kept light by Tansie Lee. It went as follows, or approximately so, depending upon the subject: "But how did you find me?" he asked.

"I knew where—and when—you'd be."

"How did you know?"

"Well, for one thing, it's history."

"Yeah," he drawled, "but whose?"

"The unwritten history of the no-world." She laughed.

"Balderdash."

"Well," she said. "We do not exist; we are not really here. Therefore the history of our lives is also figmentary. It doesn't exist."

"No?"

"Nope," she said with a shake of her head. "Nothing is real."

"Then how do you read facts out of an unreal book?"

"How do you multiply a real unit by an imaginary number?"

"We do it— Oh nuts."

"Okay," she laughed. "It'll all come out in the wash. Lunch?"

"Lunch!" he said firmly.

He led her to the galley and rummaged idly into the cabinets. In one he found a bottle that smelled inviting. "Will this," he asked, holding it up and sloshing the amber fluid in the bottle, "give we unreal people unreal hangovers?"

"It depends," she told him, opening the refrigerator and handing him a tray of ice cubes.

"Depends," he said ruminatively, busily mixing, "upon the truth of positives and negatives. A real person with an unreal hangover might not feel it any more than I can feel an object that doesn't exist simultaneously. Similarly, we unreal people might not notice a real hangover. But if we unreal folks get unreal hangovers by drinking unreal whiskey, it might hurt. Is that it? Is that what it depends on?"

She took the proffered glass. "Nope," she said, looking at him over the rim of her glass. "It just depends—like as usual—upon how much of this stuff you think you can pack away."

They stopped after lunch, parked the vehicle in a grove of trees and went out for a walk.

"I note that things are single," said Ackerman.

"Wrong," she said. "Look again. Down."

He looked down. Down—through the hard earth to where there was another surface at least fifty miles below. Another ground—plane, dim, unreal, but like the one upon which they stood.

"Why?" he asked her.

"Your explosion was minute, as cosmic powers go. But this is many years later. The most minute deviation will make a difference in displacement after a hundred years. You, my sweet, are a Man Who Moves Worlds." The capital letters were implied by her tone, and the affectionate term seemed to come naturally.

It pleased Ackerman. Tansie was an attractive girl. She was as lost in the middle of the "time-lines" as he was. Friendship—even love—might come swiftly under attractive isolation, but Ackerman believed that neither the isolation nor the length of time had been great enough yet. The attractiveness was admittedly there.

And something in the back, ignored-because-it-was-unpleasant, part of his mind was telling him, vainly, to watch out because this was entirely too idyllic.

ACKERMAN clapped a lid down on the malcontent thought and reached for Tansie's hand to help her up over a fallen log.

He retained her hand after help was no longer necessary; he liked it. The pleasant contact crowded out the wonder if on the other existence, miles away, had a similar fallen log.

He cast a sidelong look at her, and caught her watching him. They both stopped and faced one another.

Tansie stood there proudly, facing him, waiting. He fumbled mentally for a moment and then blurted: "Tansie. Tansie, what is all this?"

She smiled wistfully. "Not yet," she said. "It all must be. I—am not to tell you yet. And—Les—I'd prefer, even so, not to spoil it."

"Spoil it?" he exploded. "My idea is to get whatever trouble there is to be over with so that I can take the rest of whatever time there is for me to know you better."

"You'll have a lifetime," she promised. "Providing you are a completely free agent. My dear, this way I am sure of the future. One small slip, and the future is changed. You—"

"Baloney!"

Tansie took a step towards him. "Forget it." Her eyes were inviting—He looked into them; Ackerman, in thirty years of life, had never before met the girl whose eyes drew him so.

He reached for her, and Tansie came willingly into his arms. He thought briefly that Tansie could make him forget anything—and was proven right; he forgot even that.

CHAPTER THREE

SECONDS, or seven thousand years later, a rough laugh broke it up. Tansie hurled herself away from him, whirling out of his arms. The other was facing them less than ten yards away.

"Very pretty," he said with heavy scorn. "Very pretty." He waved at them with a carbine. "So the great physicist, the hope of the civilized world, ultimate founder of the galactic empire, is found lollygagging with a broad."

"Listen—" snarled Ackerman. He lunged forward, blind with anger. The loud *crack!* of the rifle brought his head up, and the bullet smacked the ground between his feet.

"What's the matter?" asked the other with an oily voice. "You object to my term? Well...Tansie, you tell him."

Tansie shook her head, dazedly. "You can't say—"

"No?" snapped the other. "Well, I'll tell him, Tansie. Ackerman, your gal-friend is married."

"No—!" cried Tansie in a voice of mingled pain and terror. She was cut off by another crack of the carbine.

Tansie looked at the other man. "Calvin Blaine, you're not—"

"Ackerman is coming with me," said Blaine.

"I don't think so," Les told him.

Blaine laughed cheerfully. "You haven't much to say about this."

Les spat in the other's direction. "Don't let me get within grabbing distance of that gun," he told Blaine. Disdainfully, he turned his back and faced Tansie.

"Is it true?"

She looked at Blaine.

Blaine said, in a cold voice, "Tell him the truth. Tansie—or I'll kill *him.*"

Ackerman turned again. "Truth?" he sneered. "Truth at the point of a gun? 'Truth' in this case is forcing Tansie to make a statement that you approve. Truth! Bah!"

Tansie looked at Ackerman, then at Blaine; this was an event she had not counted on. Tansie had believed that the history she knew—unwritten but known—was truth, despite its happening in the future respective to "Real Time." She had been wondering about predestination and the resulting futility of all effort; this seemed to prove to her that this nebulous life was still subject to change at the whim of chance. But Ackerman was important, and even though his definition of truth was correct in this case, he must not be destroyed.

She looked at Blaine and then at Ackerman—the collapse of all her hopes had stricken her dumb.

Tears were close to the surface. Tears for herself, for her hopes—and for Les Ackerman. Yet there was a chance. Les must not be destroyed, even at the expense of her own life; Blaine knew that, which was why he threatened Ackerman instead of her.

Calvin Blaine lifted the carbine.

Les Ackerman measured his chances and decided against them, for the moment at least.

With hidden tears stinging her eyes, Tansie Lee held up her left hand. Ackerman looked down and saw it. Very plain, very formal, as lacking in surface glitter as Tansie had seemed—Les wondered whether the simple serenity of the wedding ring was as false a cover for cheap green brass as—as—

You damned fool! he told himself. *You trebly underlined, capital-lettered idiot! A soft glance, warm lips, and an almost-invitation—and you forget yourself!*

The blind, stupid haze cleared from Ackerman's bewildered mind and he looked into Tansie Lee's face. She had been looking at him, searching his face carefully. But she had seen his expression, and was turning away. Ackerman watched her go, coldly. *A fool,* he said to himself, *is a man who makes the same mistake twice!*

Tansie walked away, her shoulders down, her warmly rich figure gaunt, and the line and soul of dejection.

CALVIN BLAINE coughed and said: "Sorry, Ackerman. This is mostly for self-defense. I knew she'd work on you very well before I got to you—and I knew that she'd work well enough to drive you into blind fury at the first mention of her perfidy."

"I don't understand all of this," said Ackerman. His voice was hard and his attitude one of complete indifference. "What's going on, anyway?"

"You've heard of two countries, or two men fighting for their lives?"

"Yes."

"Ackerman, you started this. Unwittingly, of course. Bombardment of Element X—which we call Temperon—produced a freak field of force that caused a division in the universal stream of time. It has never happened before and it will never happen again according to the probabilities—no one knows what happened.

"This, Ackerman, produced a twin existence. Two probabilities that stem from a dual explosion in your laboratory. In one, there was a complete success to your work; in the other, there was total destruction of your effort. Not only did you split the world into twin existences through 'time', Ackerman, but you also split it definitely into twin camps of reasoning. Your work was based upon findings that came from countries that were enemies not many years before. Figuratively, you stood on the shoulders of scientific wisdom to prepare your manuscript of facts on the element Temperon.

"Your work was an indictment of any policy that would hamstring the free interchange of ideas, concepts, work, and success. It was living proof that all men contribute to the advancement of civilization whether they be good, not so good, bad, quick, dead, friend or one-time enemy.

"The other existence, however, has your evidence that men were plodding through the uncharted seas of boundless energy and power—"

"But I was not!" stated Ackerman.

"You know that and your fellows know it. But your scientific fellows are a minority, and many of them doubt their own figures. They know only that *something* blew you and your laboratory off of the face of the earth, and they all wonder why—even those who claim to *know* that you were working with nothing dangerous.

"Therefore, Ackerman, because you and your kind were obviously playing with a field of work that might cause the destruction of the universe, research is throttled and controlled to within an inch of its life. There is no leaping from an unfounded theory to cold mathematics to foregone conclusion like a fast double play from short to second to first. To bombard a ten milligram sample of anything never before bombarded, the scientist must make ten ten-hour bombardments, adding one milligram each time."

"Well—where do I come in?" asked Ackerman.

"You have the answer to mankind's life in your brain," replied Blaine. "We need your help."

"That's about what Tansie Lee was telling me." Ackerman's mind underwent a very brief session of self-denunciation at the thought of Tansie.

"I'll show you," he said. "My ship is nearby. I'll show you, Ackerman, the destruction of a solar system by men who know too little about the stuff with which they work."

Ackerman shrugged uncertainly. "I'm not Solomon, nor even one of his seventh-assistant helpers," he said thoughtfully. "But it strikes me that there is as much danger letting everybody play with atomic fire as there is in throttling all brainwork."

Blaine laughed heartily. "Any kind of fire," he said between shouts of admiring laughter. "Even firewater! They tried complete prohibition once and people started to make everything from Allyl Acetate to xylylene glycol in their cellars! No one yet has thought of legislation forcing everybody to swizzle a quart a day, and even the flushest of lushes doesn't offer drinks to kids. No, Ackerman, you're to be proven correct."

"Why?"

"That's partly why we need your help," said Blair. "People have been bootlegging science to a dangerous degree. In the other existence, people have been taking a free and untrammeled holiday. In the future to which we're going, you'll see the answer. Men have learned the folly of fighting one another, Ackerman, but they have also learned the way across the strait of 'time'. Burning up my world by atomics will not cause their own world to die."

"Doesn't that give them both a future?"

Blaine clapped Ackerman on the shoulder and smiled sorrowfully. "They cannot cross materially," he said. "They can blast only with energy, yet, even so, there is jealousy, hate, and malice. Remember this, Lester Ackerman…what man cannot conquer, man destroys…"

CALVIN BLAINE'S ship was about the same as Tansie's. Blaine motioned Ackerman in and followed, closing the door. From the controls, up in the pilot's deck, came a musical voice that struck a chord in Ackerman's mind: "You found him, dad?"

"My daughter," said Blaine unnecessarily. She came to meet them; a golden blonde with sparklingly mischievous eyes, upturned corners of a round, rich mouth that was also generous, and a warmly tanned skin.

"This is him, Laurie. Ackerman, my daughter, Laurie Blaine."

"How do you do, Miss Blaine."

"I do fine, usually," she told him with a laugh. "And I start at once; you are to call me Laurie; I'll eschew formality, too, and call you Les." She turned to her father. "Are we off in the planned direction?"

"We are. I succeeded in getting to them before any damage was done."

"Soon enough?" asked Laurie with a devilish glint in her eye. Ackerman squirmed uncomfortably, wishing he could duck the double entendre.

Calvin Blaine recognized the possibility of Ackerman's discomfort—possibly because Blaine was no more perfect than anyone else. He would never tell Laurie that he had interrupted a love scene; she would never know unless Ackerman blurted it out.

He nodded negligently. "He didn't know who she was," he said.

Laurie smiled at Ackerman. "We know that Les Ackerman is a shy man," she said. "It—is becoming. But to tell you the truth, Les, I'd be worried about a bronze statue if that woman decided to hurl herself at its head."

The way Laurie said *that woman* was of the same one that one uses in describing someone who was violating the no-spitting ordinance in the subway.

"You're still pure and simple?" she asked him with a laugh.

"I'm simple, anyway."

"Good; I'm not too bright in some things. Dad's tried to tell me about Temperon. I'm baffled; what's Temperon?"

ACKERMAN took a deep breath and was frankly glad to get off of the tender subject of his affections and onto a more stable discussion of material physics.

"It's an involved yarn," said Ackerman. Back in the nineteen-thirties, a scientist by the name of Enrico Fermi was successful in bombarding almost every element with neutrons, and succeeded in most cases by raising the atomic number of most of them. The neutron, you see, enters the nucleus, making the nuclear mass too great for the charge. The nucleus then re-establishes stability over a time by emitting a beta particle, transforming, in effect, one of the neutrons to a proton. Now the top of the periodic chart is uranium, and Fermi wondered what he would get if he tried to raise the top-number."

"That was plutonium?" asked Laurie.

"Neptunium first, then plutonium. After the Second War, science took up, again, investigating for the sake of learning more about their surroundings. Plutonium was top number for not too long. Element ninety-five came next, and ninety-six followed soon. We were working on element number one hundred and forty-four; that is the one called Temperon."

"There are that many elements above the former top?"

"There are, theoretically, an infinite number of elements. Most of the top elements are unstable—that is, radioactive. Fissionable elements occur more and more frequently in the top brackets. No one has ever seen element one hundred and eight, you know; it fissions automatically as soon as it is made."

"How do you hurdle it, then?"

"Bombard it with deuterons, which raises the charge one number and the mass two numbers. It isn't easy, but it works." He looked at Laurie with curiosity. For an avowed lack of education in atomics, Laurie knew the proper questions to ask. He wondered whether her interest was as great or her desire for knowledge as deep as she said—or whether she was doing her best to put him at ease by leading him into talk about the subject he liked best.

Then, surprisingly, she looked him in the eye and winked with a brazen leer. She stood up and headed for the kitchen, knowing that he would follow. When he arrived, she was busily mixing drinks. He smiled. It was an excellent grade of scotch; he said so.

The drink relaxed him.

Laurie took the third drink in to her father. "Good for the soul," he said to Ackerman, lifting the glass.

"It is," he said heartily.

Then Calvin Blaine drew Ackerman's story out. Blaine was genuinely interested in the true history of the world, and enjoyed listening to Ackerman's description of the events' that took place during World War II and afterwards.

"First hand telling", said Blaine; "It held cards, spades, and big casino over the books." The drinks helped Ackerman to relax, and before he knew it, the aroma of fine steak was filling the ship.

Laurie, too, was an excellent cook.

CHAPTER FOUR

"IT WAS," said Les Ackerman as he awoke, "an eventful sixty hours since the eventful partial explosion on the laboratory." And in twenty six hours since Tansie Lee had found him at six o'clock the previous morning, Les had traveled a several of hundred years and a good many millions of miles in space.

Not bad, he thought, *for someone who does not exist.*

He stretched and turned over for another forty winks, and was dozing when the door opened and Laurie Blaine came in with coffee, which she held temptingly under his nose until he reached for it, and then held completely out of reach.

"Come and get it," she said mischievously.

"I don't dare," he laughed.

"How will I know that you're getting up?" she asked suspiciously.

"Take my word for it; that smells like tomorrow morning."

"Well," she said brightly, "in case you're interested, this is tomorrow morning. Get up!"

"You get out and I'll get up," he told her.

Then from the doorway, Calvin called: "Better; we're not long nor far from the scene I want to show you."

"Good enough for me," replied Ackerman. "Drag that woman out of here, will you?"

"Come on, shameless wench," laughed Blaine to his daughter. "Despite your arguments, modesty is a virtue. Let the man get dressed in peace." He grinned at Les. "She'd sit there and make snide remarks about your knees," he said. "Git!" he told her.

She got. And Les was thoroughly awake and dressed in minutes.

After breakfast, Blaine took the controls himself. "We'll watch this from a distance," he said. "I've enough power to break away from the temporal inertia and attractive mass. We can see both sides of this thing, which is more than those doing it can see."

There was the feeling of lift to the vehicle. It went on for an hour, through the gray haze that pressed against the windows of the ship while they were in motion. Then, finally, Blaine turned from the controls and the haze cleared.

"I've accelerated the 'time-rate'," he said. "Now that we're out of Earth's attractive temporal field."

"Why?"

"Destruction of anything the size of the Earth takes time," explained Blair. "I've read stories in which the Earth crashed into another planet, and it took place in a matter of minutes. Forgetting that at planetary velocities—Earth is about seventeen miles per second orbital, if I remember correctly— it takes Earth over a minute to cover one diameter of motion. Also the chances of a real crash, like a couple of golf balls colliding is impossible."

"Roche's Limit?" asked Ackerman. "They'd start to come apart by mutual gravitational attraction before they hit, and the resulting crash would be more like two spoonsful of baking powder hitting one another."

"Sounds messy," said Laurie.

Ackerman looked cheerfully sour. "It would be," he told her.

"This affair is not to be that simple," stated Blaine. "No collision. Just beamed energy. Equally messy, though."

"The 'time' speed-up is obvious, isn't it?" asked Les, looking at the distant Earth through the telescope. I can definitely perceive the turning."

"We're running free at about twenty to one," said Blaine. "Earth will turn once in about an hour and twelve minutes."

"When does the big show start?"

"Any moment now."

"But…but where's the green hazy fog?" asked Les. "I thought—"

"That fog is only apparent when near a body like Earth. It is caused by the diffraction of the air—you see, when you're moving through 'time', the speed-up of air-motion causes a complete diffraction and diffusion of all light. We're in space where there is no air."

AS BLAINE spoke, a twinkle of light burst like an exploding bomb a half diameter to the north of the Earth. The speckle of light spread and diminished in intensity; it still cast a baleful but momentary glow over the Northern Hemisphere—or not-quite-hemisphere because of its proximity to Earth.

"That's the beginning," said Blaine.

Minutes later, a second pinprick of energy expanded. This one was either on the surface or very close; it was hard to tell which. But the effect was terrible. A ruddy gout of multicolored smoke and flame spurted out, leaping from the point of contact. It raced up and away from the surface making a tiny tuft of fluffy smoke that looked like a wisp of cotton pulled through the cloth covering of a pillow. It was tiny compared to the size of Earth, but the shock wave that raced in a concentric circle away from the gout of energy— racing across the ground in a crawling distortion—was quite visible. Its amplitude died as it spread until it was invisible.

Minutes later, a contracting circle of shock wave appeared. It converged and closed down on the spot that was still covered by the tiny cloud. There was considerable amplitude at that spot where all the energy returned, then the concentric shock wave raced away From the point again.

"I'd like to see the antipodes," muttered Ackerman.

"We'll see others," Blaine promised.

"That was the same shock wave, wasn't it?" Laurie wanted to know.

"Yes," said her father, watching through his telescope. "It started from that city and spread out across the Earth. On the other side, of course, the thing converged to zero, passed through itself and spread out again. It returned to its origin—and will continue to encircle Earth until it dies. Each time it is less perfect because of wave-diffraction and refraction due to a non-homogenous medium. That tends to spread it out, makes its focal point imperfect. Its energy will be dissipated in heat due to resistance. It will eventually die and—"

"Here comes one!" exploded Laurie. "From the other side."

They watched. The shock wave converged, growing in amplitude as it circled down to the pinpoint. There was a clouding at the focal point where Earth itself ground itself to bits in the grip of a transmitted wave of energy. The receding wave spread out again.

Then, as though the enemy had been searching out their target—bracketing it—other pinpricks burst in widely separated places. The crisscrossing of concentric shock waves cast up high peaks that raced along, tearing up the very ground.

"On Earth," said Blaine, "nine hours have passed since the initial blast."

More time passed, and then with the target accurately bracketed, the pinpricks of energy burst again and again and again in lightning speed. The face of Terra sparkled; scintillated. The ground writhed and boiled; mighty gouts of earth and tortured stone burst upward where the bursts of power drove below the surface. The scintillating face of the earth increased to a constant glow as the ferocity of the attack increased. Moving clouds of gray and white obscured the surface, through which came the angry, flaming glow of surface bombing by high, sheer energy.

The color temperature of the Cloud increased until the scintillating, ever-changing illumination changed subtly. Now the smoky, cloudy earth shone with an angry glow more bright than the individual sparkles; it was like a fog-cloud illuminated from behind. "The Earth," said Blaine in an awesome voice, "is growing incandescent."

ACKERMAN took a deep breath. "And still," he sighed bitterly, "they continue!"

"They will continue, until they raise the temperature of the Earth so high that the thermal energy is sufficient to exceed the escape velocity of the Earth's mass. Then, driven by the Dower of the light-output, the Earth will disperse in a cloud of streaming, incandescent gas. For," Blaine added sardonically, "as the first quantities start to leave, the mass diminishes and the escape velocity diminishes also. The Earth will expand in white-hot gas and disperse forever."

"Horrible," said Les Ackerman through a dry and aching throat.

He turned from the telescope and faced Calvin Blaine. "I—started this?"

Blaine nodded, but added: "Unwittingly. No fault of yours."

"Then, what can I do to avert it?"

"You must help us," said Blaine. "Will you?"

"I'll do anything. But if this is an extension of 'Time', how can the future be changed?"

"This is just a most certain probability; intervention may change it."

Ackerman sat down weakly, and was thankful for the oversized jolt of scotch that Laurie handed him. "I'm still puzzled; it seems to me that this splitting-off in 'time' must go on constantly. A tree might grow either to the left or to the right. Do not these offer different world-line endings?"

"By and large," said Blaine, "they do. But you must remember that most incidents are unimportant to the complex. We have two living possibilities due to your unfortunate accident. You see, Ackerman, it is true that a tree may grow either to the left or to the right. It does not grow both ways. When the 'time' comes for the decision to be made, the forces that work toward causing that decision have been in force for some duration and the tree takes the most logical move; therefore only one future ensues. Even in the decision of a possible dictator of all humanity, the decisions he makes are dependent upon his past experience. Grand Chance is not a matter of tossing dice; men have a free will, Ackerman. Yet their lives are fairly well cast ahead of time by the course of their pasts. The formula that caused World War II to grow out of World War I was evident enough to prevent World War III; yet in no way could Adolph Hitler have been averted because he rose out of a situation already created."

"It still sounds like predestination—and the futility of all effort."

"Not so. You are a free will, Lester—yet your actions are conditioned by your past. By 'free will', I mean you have a choice of alternatives within the frame of conditions around you. The only ones whose actions are not dictated by solid experience are the insane. And they, even by the Ancients, were termed 'Unpredictable'."

Ackerman nodded. Once you knew a man, you could make a fair prediction of how he would react to a given set of conditions, starting no major alterations in his motives and view points, etc. Perhaps if you knew him very well, your prediction would be better. Les smiled grimly. No man knew another that well.

In fact, he admitted silently, *no man knew himself well enough to predict his own reaction to an entirely unprecedented situation!*

OUTSIDE, the terrible earth-glow had become intense. It was expanding like a misshapen balloon. Wispy clouds of high-energy were fingering out into space, followed shortly by the main mass as it dispersed. It was ten times the original diameter now, and increasing rapidly.

"It will take days," said Blaine. "Of our accelerated 'time'. But you know the end-point."

Ackerman knew. The end-point of this was a blank space in the solar system and a gradual re-establishment of the energy-distribution of the solar system to make up for the missing mass-energy and attraction of the destroyed Earth.

"What can I do?" he asked helplessly.

"How did they hit the Earth?"

"I don't know," answered Ackerman.

"They had observers, just as we are. They got here by penetrating the no-world between the world-lines as we have done. We—you—must develop a means of our doing that. You, Ackerman, are really the only one in historic time who knows the secret of Temperon."

"No, I do not."

Calvin Blaine smiled tolerantly. "I am of the destroyed Earth," he said sadly. "We do not know how to penetrate the barrier."

"But you are here," said Les.

Blaine nodded very slowly. "Yes—because you, Les Ackerman, know that secret."

"But I don't—I don't!"

"You will recall it. You will work; you will succeed. And once you succeed in penetrating the secret of the barrier between the twin possibilities, you will help us. Then we will be able to come through into this temporal freedom of this unreal existence—to help you!"

Ackerman groaned. "I am the man," he said quizzically, "who travels backwards in 'time' to write himself a set of plans on how to build a 'time machine' which he is now using to deliver the letter."

"Indeed."

"And so," Laurie said, smiling, "you reach down, grasp yourself by the shoelaces, and lift."

"Ridiculous… But I will help!" Calvin Blaine caught Ackerman's hand in a firm grasp. Laurie pressed his other arm against her in a gesture of real affection. Ackerman felt, within him, the beginnings of a glow of success—

And at that precise moment the ship lurched, throwing them all off balance.

CHAPTER FIVE

CALVIN BLAINE cursed, strove to disentangle himself from Ackerman, who was trying to raise both his weight and that of Blaine from Laurie, who was pressed harshly across the heavy desk; its edge was cutting into her spine.

The lurch changed direction and hurled them all from the desk and across the tiny room against the wall. This time the combined weight of Laurie and Ackerman crushed Blaine to the wall, and drove the breath from him. He struggled weakly; Laurie slipped to the floor, gasping.

Ackerman, cushioned first by the girl and second by her father, was dizzy, but not harmed. Blaine slipped to the floor as Les Ackerman stooped and lifted the girl to her feet.

Then there was a metallic, grinding sound; shortly afterwards three men strode in and snapped handcuffs over the wrists of Laurie and Calvin Blaine.

"You're lucky," one of them said to Ackerman.

"Lucky?" snorted Ackerman. "That's what he told me when he met Tansie and me."

"You're luckier this time," laughed the leader. "I'm Barry Ford. The guy with the manacles and the policeman's outfit is Tod Laplane. He who fondles the firearm is a trigger by the name of Louis Ford. He is fortunate enough to share the same parents with me."

Louis grinned cheerfully. "Sharing a fine set of parents has but one drawback," he told Ackerman. "It requires that I acknowledge Barry as my blood brother. It shouldn't happen to a salamander, let alone a dog."

Barry smiled genially. "Well," he said, "you're luckier—and have always been in better company—than I am—and have been."

Laplane turned away from his handiwork. "Shall it be pistols and coffee at daybreak?" he laughed.

"Look," said Ackerman, interested in the horseplay but annoyed by the entire occurrence, "suppose you jokers forget your unreal animosities and tell me what's going on."

"All's fair—" said Barry Ford.

"—In love and war," finished his brother Louis.

"Is that what this is?" demanded Ackerman.

"By and large," agreed Barry. "You've just witnessed the destruction of a world; their world," he added, pointing at Laurie and Calvin Blaine. "That, I must admit, was engineered by our world." To the latter word Barry added the gesture of pointing to his brother and the other man, Laplane.

"It was not a pretty sight," snapped Ackerman; "are you going to try to justify it?"

Blaine grunted angrily. "No one can justify wanton destruction.

"Remember, Ackerman, that what you have just observed is but a close probability. Believe this because we cannot prove it right now—we will later—but we have as interesting a scene to show you concerning our world. Engineered, I might say, by Blaine and his very lovely daughter."

"He told me that I was the man who could avert that affair."

"Uh-huh," grinned Barry wolfishly. "You are. You were well on the way to averting it. Look Ackerman, how long do you think this unnatural splitting of the 'time stream' can continue?"

"I don't know."

"Well, not much longer. This unreal time-space comes to an end not far from here, Ackerman. The ending of time-space—this unreal existence between two probabilities ends; and he who lets the normal passage of time catch up with him is, at the end of this time-space, trapped in the natural world. That is the 'future' and will always be the future to those of us who roam this time-space in the hope of averting the tragedy. When we all have succeeded, we will all come to the end of time-space, here and not long hence, and permit ourselves to be caught up with the natural pattern of life. Your friends here—my enemies—were about to accomplish their purpose."

"Purpose?" said Ackerman trying to follow the other man's reasoning. "Is it a foul purpose to try to prevent the death of a world?"

FORD NODDED. "You, Ackerman, are destined to save the situation. Blaine and Blaine, here, were about to permit you—with them—to be caught up with the ending of this time-space. Then the brilliant Lester Ackerman would be lost to time-space forever. The real tragedy would come, but the minor tragedy that only they consider worthy, would have been averted. So long as you remain in time-space, Ackerman, the destruction of their Earth is a definite probability."

"Sounds like a good reason for leaving."

"Yes? Then listen…so long as you remain in time-space the destruction of my world is improbable."

Calvin Blaine glared, and he spoke up. "Ackerman, what he says is true, in part, because he intends to use you to develop a means of destroying my world. If you pass into the future, our own scientists will succeed first and therefore be able to destroy his world."

"You're in the middle," said Laurie in a sympathetic voice. "No matter which you do, you've got the fate of a world on your head. I believe," she added wistfully, through welling eyes, "that I might have been able to make you forget that. In fact, had it been mine to say, you'd have been spared knowing that upon your shoulders lies the decision as to which existence should be saved. It is a question that no mortal should ever be called upon to decide."

"Come," said Barry Ford to Ackerman. He ignored the girl's plea. "We've got to get out and into our own ship. This one is drifting toward the end of time-space; we'll be caught."

"Even now," said Laurie in a voice that wrenched Ackerman's heart, "I could ease the hurt; make you forget that such a problem once was yours. He'll leave us to drift, Les. We'll be caught and taken from this life. If you decide—please come. To—me?"

Barry turned roughly and snapped: "You'd sell yourself for your world?"

"It would not be a difficult sale," she answered.

"But a bargain hard to keep pure," he snorted.

Laurie smiled. "It often happens," she said with a ring of sincerity, "that duty and logic both direct one toward his heart's desire; that's when life is best."

"And you?" Barry scowled.

"I find neither duty nor logic to be odious terms," she said; "and I'm not one to abandon a pleasant idea just because it isn't original with me."

Louis Ford suddenly jumped. "Hurry!" he shouted. "She's stalled us to the danger point!"

"Trickstress," scorned Barry.

"They lie!" screamed Laurie. "Lester—believe me!"

Calvin Blaine turned to her. "Les will do as *he* believes," he said. "And all is not lost. We may yet win; remember— this, too, if but probability!"

Louis Ford and Tad Laplane grabbed Les Ackerman by the arms and hurried from the ship, into theirs. Les heard Laurie's fading voice crying through sobs for him to stay.

THE DOOR of the other ship rapped shut and cut off the cries. "A consummate actress," said Barry levelly.

Ackerman turned to him. "I presume that Tansie Lee is one of your crowd? Frankly, I really don't know who to believe."

Barry laughed shortly. "Tansie Lee? She is none of my crowd; she's a weak-minded sitter on the temporal fence, Ackerman. She believes that both worlds can be saved."

"Well, can't they?"

"Oh, now look, Ackerman, you're not the same kind of wishy-washy creature. Life is a struggle always. Kill or be killed still works—and always will."

"Just destruction for the sake of," said Ackerman harshly, "is untenable—even though you indulge in self-justification by believing that life is always kill or be killed."

"Let's face it," said Barry Ford. "Before your perilous experiment, we had a single world, with a single 'future'. You caused fission of 'time'. The twin existences are starting to converge again; the energy used in splitting 'time' is dissipating and as it is converted, the time-streams converge. But they have not been the same world for hundreds of years. What will happen when suddenly the solar system contains two suns, two Earths, and two of each planet? The sky will be filled with double stars where single stars once were, and quadruple stars where doubles now exist. Some, which have not moved far from one another in their contingent existences, will find one another occupying the same space! See?"

Ackerman scowled uncertainly. "It looks to me as though we're scheduled for a big blast anyway."

Ford shook his head with a slight smile. "Nope," he said. "Not at all. You see, Ackerman, there is only one thing that tends to draw the coincident existences together. One force against the fissioning force of your little experiment. If we can destroy that force, the twin lives will continue to drift apart."

"And that force?"

"That force, Ackerman, is the physical energy of the human mind!"

"Uncontrolled? What is the affinity?"

Barry bit his lip and shrugged. "Human cussedness," he said. "Why, fundamentally, are you a brilliant physicist?"

"I'm not; and I've been called that by too many people."

"You are and we'll pursue the question. Why?"

Ackerman grinned. "Just ape-like curiosity," he said. "I like to know what makes things tick."

"Research," said Barry, "revealed to our world that this 'time-split' did obtain. It was announced. Instantly all people began to wonder what the other one looked like, whether he had a 'time-brother' on the other one, and every man, woman, and child found himself hoping, someday, to join the other world. Doubtless those of the other Earth did likewise."

Ackerman nodded absently. "You can destroy the Earth but you can't change human nature, is that it?"

"With precision."

ACKERMAN thought for a moment. Then he said: "I'm in the middle; I've been told by three groups that within my mind lies the hope of salvation. That may be so, but where it lies I'll be unable to tell until someone tells me. Maybe I'll meet myself here in time-space. Then perhaps I can tell me." He laughed bitterly.

"However," he said roughly, "I'm still in the middle. I've been led around both by the nose and by emotions and logic that may be corrector sheer sophistry. Someone should haul off and tell me the truth, the whole truth, and nothing but; too many people seem to be keeping things to themselves. Like the gang who is afraid to vote for a square deal because a square deal means that they'd get what was coming to them and they know they wouldn't like what they deserved.

"Everyone seems more than willing to make use of me to further their own ends. I'm still in the middle because I don't know the whole story.

"However again," he said with a sour smile, "there is one item upon which all warring groups agree. And that, gentlemen, is that Lester Ackerman's mind contains the answer to the problem. Until I know what the answer is, I'm unable to help friend or foe, or in between. Nor," he added, "do I know which is which, yet.

"Therefore," he finished, "I'll go along with you because you happen to have captured the pawn in free gambit; perhaps I'll learn the answer to all of my questions at the same time."

Barry and Louis Ford and Tod Laplane listened quietly. Then Barry nodded. "You've been pulled this way and that way, Ackerman, because you were unable to move on your own; it is an admission of weakness to refuse the other side its due. It is an admission of strength, belief in one's own ideals, and faith in the rightness of himself if he is not only willing for the other side to be heard, but urges it. Well, Ackerman, we think we're right and we'll take you at your word; we have every reason to believe that our side of this complicated story is the soundest."

"Then how do I start?"

Barry smiled. "We all need a means of entering time-space from a real existence; you are the only one able to do it so far."

"But you're here."

"We are—but excellent probabilities; we are proof that you succeeded. You might fail, Ackerman, and then our life would remain on our individual worlds. Our life here will fade and all we've been able to do will also disappear."

"And me?" asked Les, puzzling. "Am I a real identity, wandering through an unreal realm of fancy?"

"This is an unreal world," said Barry thoughtfully. "Therefore you must be unreal, too. However, if you fail, it will be as though you died in that explosion. If you succeed, you will live again. With us!"

CHAPTER SIX

BARRY FORD, unlike Les Ackerman's other companions, was set up for work. Tansie had wanted to show him first and explain afterwards; what her real purpose was, Les Ackerman could not divine. He suspected her motives deeply; after all, Tansie was a married woman by her own admission, a fact she had not mentioned until it had been forced from her. Not only that, but she had behaved like a woman who was not only interested in him but who also wanted his interest in her. Ackerman squirmed uncomfortably as he recalled his complete, dog-like faith. He'd missed the ring; it was small and of natural gold that blended with Tansie's golden skin. He suspected that she had been careful to keep her left hand either out of sight or in motion, so that he could not see it.

The Blaines at least, were more straightforward; there was less mystery to them. Or, he admitted, their purpose had been uncovered by Barry Ford and Company. At least there seemed to be no perfidy there. Laurie was justified in trying to save her own Earth. It was a rather involved question, one that might never be solved. Ackerman might never be sure whether Laurie's interest was real. Saving a world was a large item, one that might drive a person into most any devious act. He had no doubt that Laurie was a consummate actress, as Barry Ford claimed. Calvin Blaine was equally justified. Ackerman smiled grimly. He saw no reason to vote for one against the other; he did not subscribe to their policy, which was to save their own at whatever expense to any other, yet he was firm in his own willingness to admit that they were justified in their own minds. Placed in a similar position, Ackerman knew that he would lie, cheat, and steal to save his own Earth from destruction.

But things were clearer. Ackerman held no illusions now. He pegged Barry Ford right. Ford, of course, was smart; he knew that by this time there could be little chance for blind leading. His sensible course was to admit the conflict and ask Ackerman to view both sides before acting. Also, grinned Ackerman, Barry Ford was smart enough to realize that after having two women hurled at him, Les would be inclined to view any other such acts as sheer folly. The adage said: Once burned, twice shy. After twice scorched, how skittish for the third time?

He had completed the circle of thought; he was back to Barry Ford. The third party in this wild game was, unlike the others, set up for laboratory investigation; Les admitted once that he did net know about Tansie Lee and the Blaines. Maybe they were also set up. He hadn't been around that long.

Les Ackerman was beginning to understand the basis for the famed General Semantics. It was fine to know what was "truth," or feasible, or "good." It was even better to know what was not truth, or good, or feasible; that implied a greater recognition of knowledge. Thomas Edison was reported to have known several thousand things about his nickel storage battery that would not work.

The trouble with Ackerman, he himself realized, was that he knew nothing at all. It was an insane program; he was here, aided and working for men who were able to get here because Les had been successful in his work. And then they blithely stated, coldly and calmly, that so soon as he proved himself unable to succeed, they would all disappear!

He shook his head, and then grinned. Fervently he prayed that this was not a wild dream; it was such a fearful mess that any waking would be a sorry anticlimax. He recalled Doctor Forbes, the eminent psychiatrist, who once said that there was absolutely no way to prove to one's own satisfaction that he was either dreaming or awake. He remembered that especially because he'd had a dream shortly afterwards in which he dreamed that he had just awakened from a dream. Doctor Forbes had nodded when told, had mentioned that his subconscious had used that method to try to prove to his dreaming mind that the dream was real.

He stopped thinking along those lines. That way madness lay. It was reminiscent of the childlike reasoning that asks: "But Daddy, who brings the baby storks?"

Or, he reconsidered irrelevantly, how many angels can stand on the point of a pin.

THERE WAS another, more pertinent thing. On that point, Ackerman left his room and went to Barry Ford. "Look, Barry," he said. "I want to know how *you* got here."

"You brought us through."

"And where is the equipment I used?"

Barry shook his head. "I don't know right now."

"And I suppose that the Blaines came likewise?"

Barry nodded.

Les Ackerman shook his head. "I've been shoved around, so much that I see little reason in bringing this gang through so that you can all shove me around. I'd like to go back myself."

"You can never go back," said Barry, sincerely. "And you'll find that living in this time-space is not the bed of roses it might seem. It gets god damn lonesome. You'll get wild for the touch of an honest whim. We bring through only what we plan ahead for; you must plan every item, Ackerman, which leaves the chance-factor of living completely out. There is no getting up in the middle of the night to take a run to the corner drugstore for a cup of coffee. Or calling up your girl for a quick date as a pleasant surprise. If you hope to do something like that, you've got to plan it ahead and say to yourself: *'On the seventieth evening in* time-space, *I shall surprise my beloved by presenting her with—something very unperishable.'* I'm sorry that I cannot help you, Ackerman."

"You might have brought the equipment through with you."

"Or a model? No go, Ackerman; the thing isn't like a radio set or a small cyclotron. It's more a matter of force fields and energy gradients, as I too—vaguely understand it."

"Why didn't anybody think to ship through a physicist?"

Ford snapped the communicator on and called: "Fellows, come here, all of you!"

Louis Ford came first, and Tod Laplane. Then a striking brunette that Ackerman had not seen before—and for whom Barry said, quickly: "This is Tod's sister Joan; she's here as a general statistician and recorder, and not for the purpose of enticing you."

"That's not very complimentary to either of us," said Ackerman.

Joan smiled honestly. "No, it isn't. But it is true, Lester. You see, I'm a gatherer of facts; I know how people have been trying to use you. I promise—we will not."

Tod smiled at her and then asked: "Why the general call, Barry?"

Barry grinned. He gave them a brief resume of the talk and discussion, and Ackerman's questions of why it couldn't be done by copying the models used to bring them through. Then, with a flourish and a beautifully executed counterfeit of Lester Ackerman's voice, tone, and diction, said: "Why didn't anybody think to ship through a physicist?"

Laughter rang through the ship. Barry himself broke down and leaned weakly against the desk. Tod Laplane fell inert into a chair and shook with gales of silent laughter. Louis Ford merely gulped inanely, and Joan added her mirth in a gurgling contralto.

"Okay," snapped Ackerman, "so soon as I find the face I dropped here somewhere, I'll leave."

That stopped the laughter. "Look, Ackerman, *you're* the great physicist; why should we have another?"

Ackerman snorted. "The next character who calls me a 'great physicist' either with or without capital letters is going to get a mouthful of fist," he snarled; "I'm tired of being the main point in a joke."

Barry sobered quickly. "It is not used in a sense of ridicule or insult."

"I don't give a damn how it's used. I don't like a lot of people calling me a veritable messiah. I'd not like it even if their tongues weren't shoved eight miles out in their cheeks. So stop it, unless you'd like to go a few swift ones with me."

Barry nodded. "Sorry, Ackerman. But—you do understand—we know you brought us here. Within your own mind and your own ability, you have the secret to the big question."

"About all I know about the physics of this business is that it started with a few grams of Temperon."

"We'll get you some Temperon," said Barry. "And a cyclotron. And most anything else you're likely to need."

"Good," snorted Ackerman. "Get me a lie detector; eight gallons of scopolamine; and a psychiatrist—and have 'em comb my mind. Frankly, I'd like to know the answer, too."

*   *   *

ACKERMAN settled for the cyclotron and the Temperon. He spent a week of trying, but little came of it according to him. Barry Ford had come well prepared. The mass spectrograph was a beaut; the cyclotron was a physicist's dream; and the physico-chemical laboratory must have set someone back a cold half billion.

And to top it all, Ackerman had been the mainspring that brought it through, and was now trying to figure out how and why.

He learned more about the nuclear properties of Temperon. They were nothing to get excited about, or he considered them normal until the statistician-girl, Joan Laplane looked up from her notes and asked, innocently: "Temperon is stable. The neutron-isotope—making it the next atom-number above, is radioactive. But I note that it is doubly radioactive."

"It is. It either emits an alpha particle and drops two numbers and four masses down, or emits a beta ray and jumps a number up with no change in mass. In the first case the resultant is stable. In the second case, the resultant then emits an alpha particle and an electron and becomes stable— the same element."

"But why should it emit one of two particles?"

"That's a normal state for many radioactives," said Ackerman. "Radioactivity is a sign of atomic instability. The ejection of the unbalancing particle is not instantaneous. It takes 'time'. In the meantime, the nucleus is unbalanced. Now, this unbalance energy is distributed among the particles of the nucleus, and depending whether the alpha collects the necessary energy first or whether the random rambling of this energy drives out a beta ray, we have the splitting of the radioactive ladder. It happens, for instance, in all three of the normal radioactive chains: Thorium, actinium, and uranium. Thorium drops down the scale normally, dropping alpha particles and beta rays until it reaches Thorium C, which is an isotope of bismuth—bismuth 212. There it splits into Thorium C' or Thorium C". Thorium C' emits alpha and becomes lead 208; Thorium C" emits a beta ray and—likewise—becomes lead 208."

"Might it mean an unknown structure of the nucleus?" she asked.

"Might," he said reflectively. "There's isotopes-elements with the same atomic number but different masses. There are isobars—elements with the same atomic masses but different numbers. Maybe there's you-name-it-bars with similar masses and numbers but different structures."

"Different meson activity."

"Mesobars?" he laughed; "I'll buy that." It intrigued him, and he went on: "Maybe Temperon, in splitting into two different possible atoms, produces a situation whereby the reactions between the two elements results in something new in nuclear physics."

Barry Ford looked up and said: "I could see that it might be messy if Element X fissioned into radio-iodine and radio-phosphorus."

"Not phenomenally so," replied Ackerman, shaking his head. "A few atoms of explosive chemical mixture is still small peanuts to the energy of a radioisotope, let along a true fission. And the resulting chemical combination still has the radioisotopes in it, which will emit and change. Chemical combination of an atom of hydrocarbon and oxygen produces a few electron volts. Alpha from any radioisotope runs into millions of electron volts."

"Um. Well, what have you got?"

"I don't know," said Ackerman; "I've got to think."

He stood up and stretched, and said he was going for a walk. Idly, he hefted the bombarded Temperon on his fingers and then dropped it into a side pocket. He turned and left the laboratory.

IT WAS ON Earth, of course, set in the back hills of Wisconsin, several miles from Ladysmith. Ackerman wanted to roam the roadways, and possibly gaze upon one of the handy lakes and wish fervently that he was not trapped in a no-world where he could do nothing but fume.

A car came up behind him, and he stopped to watch. It was not a phantom car of the real world, but a time-space car of his unreal existence. Joan Laplane leaned out. "Ride," she stated; "gets farther and leaves energy to enjoy whatever you're seeking."

"Okay," he said. "What I want to do, I guess, is to ride through a city and watch people."

"That's masochism," she told him.

"Perhaps," he nodded. "But its also a matter of frustration; I'll ride if you'll drive this hickey through traffic."

"Right through," she said with a cheerful laugh.

It was rather hair-raising to Les. The girl drove well, but downright recklessly. That is, until he remembered that they could drive through any other car in motion.

Joan Laplane drove through other cars to pass them, and at one time she enjoyed driving on the left side of the road through a careening coupe that was racing towards them. It gave Ackerman a thrill and, in a sense, helped him to relax.

Then they were in the town of Ladysmith, a minute metropolis of about ten thousand people, but large enough in relation to the other towns in the vicinity to be the county seat. Joan brazenly selected a fine parking place in between two *No Parking* signs in front of the city hall, and backed her car through the cars of two of the local politicians who were neo-politically disregarding the signs.

"That'll show 'em," she said with a grin.

"Why stop?"

"I want to dance," she told him. "We'll not pay entry, nor can we buy a drink. But we can use their floor and we can dance right through the other customers and never get an elbow in the ribs."

Ackerman laughed. This time-space had some advantages. "But if your feet get trampled, I can't blame some clumsy-footed stranger."

Joan nodded, and her raven hair rippled tantalizingly. "Nope," she said, "you can't; so if you dance on my feet I'll bark your shin with a spike heel. Fair enough?"

"Fair," he said.

CHAPTER SEVEN

WITH SMILES of mutual amusement, Joan and Les walked through the door of a small nightclub, past the hatcheck-girl, past the headwaiter, and into the clubroom. "First time," said Joan, "that anybody has ever got into a joint like this without paying well for the privilege."

"It has its disadvantages," said Ackerman; "we get no table."

"That's easy," laughed Joan. She led Les across the dance floor and seated herself on the edge of the bandstand, sitting right through the saxophone player's music stand. Ackerman sat beside her, his shoulder partway through the coronet player's knee. It was sometime later that they both noticed that they were not really sitting on the bandstand but upon something as firm at least three inches below the floor-level. It was, he was beginning to understand, a matter of temporal mass and temporal inertia—which Ackerman associated with permanence, dependability, and ponderosity. The Earth was quite permanent; it had been a functioning factor for a good many billion years. The building was more or less permanent, but far from having the permanence of a brick wall, for instance.

The music started and they danced; it was fun even though their feet moved ankle deep in the floor. The floor, of course, was polished and waxed. They were dancing on something that was less slick, but the matter of dancing in itself was enjoyable enough to reduce all discomfort to a minimum.

"I'd still like to order a drink," said Ackerman.

Joan shook her head. "I haven't a flask," she told him. Her statement was unnecessary. Her grandmother might have been able to conceal several quarts in and among the voluminosity of clothing. Joan Laplane, like most of the other girls of her day, would have been baffled to conceal a fluid ounce unless internally.

Liquor was not really necessary; Ackerman enjoyed himself. Joan was an excellent dancer and she was willingly lissome in his arms. She attracted him, and he was rapt in the enjoyment of the moment; so rapt that he noticed but gave no thought to the tickling movement against his hip.

It was neither annoying; nor pleasant; it was easily ignored. Whatever it might be, it could wait.

But as they moved across the phantom dance floor, the tickling motion increased slowly, raising its violence by degrees until it was no longer something to be put aside.

Ackerman gave it thought, then. It was, as he had subconsciously known all along, the sample of Temperon. It was, inexplicably, moving.

Ackerman watched it carefully, after that. He said nothing. Luckily, Joan Laplane was the kind of girl who dances silently, enjoying the silent communion of musical and physical pleasure. Therefore she did not notice that Lester's attention was directed more toward something else. Ackerman was glad that his dancing was good enough to perform without complete attention, otherwise he would not be able to keep his secret.

It—increased.

He noted it, smiled, and deliberately steered Joan and himself through another dancing couple. It was one way to make the desired test—to prove what he was beginning to suspect.

It had the desired result, but the aftermath was astounding.

The girl of the couple, through which Ackerman had passed, suddenly squirmed and stopped dancing. Ackerman steered Joan four quick steps away and made a graceful but swift turn so that he could look over her shoulder.

THE OTHER girl turned, took a quick bead on the man dancing behind her, and let him have the flat of her hand across his face.

At that instant, the music died in a cacophony and the chattering of the crowd died with it.

"Get fresh!" snapped the girl.

"What did I do?" asked the dumfounded man, rubbing his face.

The girl let him have her other hand on the other side of his face. "That'll tell you!" screamed the girl in a voice that would have awed Medusa the Gorgon.

Her escort, puzzled, stepped forward between the other two. "What's going on?"

"I don't know," answered the slapped one; "all of a sudden she ups and cracks me."

"Must've been a reason," snarled the man. "Out with it…"

The slapped-one's girl friend faced the insulted girl. "Free with your hands, aren't you, dearie?"

"So's he!" she snapped in return.

"So am I!" screeched the other girl.

She reached and came back with a handful of hair. The other girl raked four red furrows down the side of the hair-puller's cheek, and the battle was on.

"Get her out!" snapped the slapped man.

"G'wan," snarled the other fellow; he led with a right, crossed with a left, and was jolted with a short jab to the stomach.

That was the end. Waiters, bouncers, and general huskies converged. The orchestra leader rapped and the band started to play a Spike Jones arrangement of *After the Brawl was Over!*

"Wisconsin," chuckled Les. "Seems to offer everything!"

To Joan, the sentimental spell was broken; Ackerman sensed this, and took her by the arm, leading her towards the door. She went, chuckling over the incident. It was Ackerman who was slightly horrified; he knew that he had been the cause of the ruckus. He was also pleased at the results, and he believed that he might be able to do something with this strange element.

He found passing through the door slightly difficult. The Temperon sample in his pocket was slowed, as though a slight resistance were offered. The outer door moved slightly as he passed through it.

Joan, unknowing, drove home in the same reckless fashion. Ackerman prayed that they would meet no more careening cars; he was afraid that he might lose the sample if it caught in a swiftly moving body. This time, luck was with him.

LES ACKERMAN viewed his handiwork one week later. " 'Tis a real monkey-motion," he told himself, "but it should work."

It was a real Rube Goldberg, of the type often concocted for an especial test. Many kinds may be seen in any laboratory, working madly to life-test various operating members, dropping parts against steel plates to see how many bumps they will take before becoming useless.

This was similar, but adapted to a singular purpose.

It was a straight reciprocating motion that passed an arm containing the sample of Temperon back and forth through the trunk of a tree. The tree, of course, was in "Real Time" while the machine was in the "time-space." It would have simplified things if the tree trunk could be fastened to, but it was not; so the amount of drag was measured by the forces— back-forces—that tended to resist the motor that drove the gadget. At the end of each stroke, the arm entered a chamber that carried a radioactivity counter.

The tree was five or six miles from the laboratory, and only Ackerman knew where it was.

Ackerman, having been twice bitten, was thrice shy times ten. At this point, his own mother might have had trouble in convincing Ackerman that she meant only for his benefit.

At the end of another week, Ackerman was satisfied; he was certain. For the drag versus "time" had passed through a wide peak. The radioactivity versus "time" had been harder to unravel, for it possessed an irregular curve that Ackerman fought with for hours before it resolved sensibly into the superposition of several normal radioactivity curves.

The matching of the drag curve with one of the radio curves was simple, after that. And Les then spent another ten days figuring out which of the many resulting radioisotopes of Temperon was responsible for its extension through the barrier of time into the world of "Real Existence."

His progress after that was rapid. Barry, Louis, Tod and Joan were baffled by his actions and said so. They did see progress, and were pleased.

But they could offer no help.

What Les was doing with the Temperon sample was enigmatic to them, though he admitted that what they saw might lead them to the right answer eventually. A savage, given the knowledge only of the identification of materials and the working model, could easily reproduce a simple radio receiving set, yet he would have no idea as to the principles underlying the art. And many millions of people drive automobiles daily without the vaguest idea of the theory of the internal combustion engine.

The gloves that Ackerman made, studded with thin slices of Temperon, enabled him to move and handle objects in the world of reality. Then the machine—with its huge paraboloidal reflector coated on the inside with a thin layer of Temperon—gave Lester Ackerman his initial taste of success.

OUT IN THE forest, far from the laboratory, Ackerman focused the reflector on a log, lying ghostlike in the world of Real Time. It came through—not as an object might be passed or drawn through a curtain to drop on the inside, or as an object lifted from a pool of water, passing from one medium to the other. It merely solidified.

He picked it up, grunting with the effort, and passed one end through a tree. Satisfied, he dropped it from his shoulder.

He turned—and then turned again, startled. His ears perked, and the sound came again.

Looking through the trees—it was like trying to see through a heavy maze of plate glass, and the scene fifty yards from him was as hidden as if the woods had been truly solid.

"Don't he alarmed," said a voice.

Ackerman straightened. "Spying?"

"You've been successful, we see," replied Barry Ford, ignoring his accusation.

"So?" demanded Ackerman.

"I might point out that you happen to be working for us."

"Interesting. I have other ideas," returned Ackerman testily. "Since I happen to be responsible for all of you, I happen to think that I have the right to do as I damn well please."

While speaking, Ackerman had been remembering that he had no freedom. He would have preferred to work alone. And if this decision was to rest as it seemed upon him, he should be permitted to make his decision unaided—or untrammeled. The idea of trying to select which one of two worlds had a better right to the future was no problem to ponder while being badgered.

Furthermore, this outfit had little more to offer than the Blaines.

Ackerman nodded inwardly, then turned the projector and snapped the reversing switch.

Barry leaped forward. His brother Louis shouted angrily. Tod Laplane lifted his gun, and Joan cried out in alarm. Tod Laplane fired, aiming for the heart of Ackerman's projector.

The bullet—passed through.

Then the Laplane-Ford faction, wraithlike already, faded from view, leaving Ackerman alone.

ALONE? NOT quite. Ackerman had another watcher, who now came into view. "Very interesting," said Calvin Blaine. "But I fear that you have done that which will cause the destruction of my world, young man."

"How?" demanded Ackerman. "And I thought that you arid Laurie were trapped at the edge of time-space."

"You know my daughter?" asked Calvin Blaine in surprise. He called out, and Laurie came into view. "He knows you," said Calvin.

"Who is he. Is he Lester Ackerman?"

Ackerman put hands on hips and stared. "I am Les Ackerman," he said; "and this is beyond me."

"It is beyond me, too," said Calvin. "However, the destruction of my world is not a pleasant contemplation, Ackerman."

"I know; I've seen it."

"You have?"

"Yes," said Ackerman. "You showed it to me."

"No such thing," replied Laurie. "But we will, if you like."

Ackerman began to catch on. "You may, eventually," he said with a cryptic grin. "But tell me, how is my sending them back into their own world going to be instrumental in destroying yours?"

"Theirs is the world of free research," said Blaine. "Up to now, they know little of the true state of affairs, but once they return with the information, there will be trouble."

"I gather that if I'd kept them here, the initial knowledge would never reach that world?"

"You aren't properly acquainted with the chronological factors involved with the conservation of matter and energy," said Blaine. "When you sent them back, you sent them back to the precise instant of their leaving. In that way and in that way alone can the Real Time constancy be preserved. This time-space state is unreal, and therefore most anything can happen here. But they will return complete with all the knowledge they need to start the destruction of my world."

"Then," said Ackerman, "I shall stop them."

"You have time," said Blaine. "But first, tell me how you happen to know of us."

Ackerman explained his actions up to the point of his meeting with Tansie. At that point, both Blaines exploded: "Tansie Lee!"

"Know her?" asked Ackerman quietly.

"She is a rather headstrong woman," said Blaine. "Full of a rather pale, idealistic plan to save both worlds with danger to none."

Laurie eyed Ackerman with interest. "You know her?"

Ackerman nodded glumly.

"Interesting," replied Laurie. "Imagine a real man who knows Tansie Lee without becoming captivated by her rather lush charm."

"I don't go in for running around with married women," said Ackerman.

"You're not married?"

"No," he said.

Calvin interrupted what was getting uncomfortable to Ackerman. "What happened then?" he asked. Les explained the rest, but omitted the minute details of his interrupted love scene. He did tell them—by way of explanation—that his being in the company of Tansie Lee was due to the fact that he did not know she was married.

"I'm beginning to understand," said Blaine.

Ackerman nodded. "Go ahead," he said. "But be careful."

Laurie looked puzzled. "I don't get it."

Calvin turned to his daughter. "We've got to hurry," he said; "we've got to meet Lester Ackerman and Tansie Lee, take Ackerman to the edge of time to see the destruction of our world."

"Then it is to be destroyed?" said Laurie fearfully.

"It is only an excellent probability," said her father. "That may—it please God—be averted. Come."

CHAPTER EIGHT

ACKERMAN ran to the laboratory and climbed into another "time-vehicle." He drove it through "time" and "space" as fast as he could, returning to the forest area where he had sent the group back. Once there, he pursued a blind train forward in "time," hurrying to catch them.

Swiftly he moved, but as fast as he was, they were always lost ahead of him. In effect, their return was instantaneous, but so was his flight across the years. It was only to Ackerman that "time" seemed to hang heavily as he drove futureward, stopping at regular intervals to see through the gray hue that covered up the outside when the vehicle was in motion.

At long last he saw them, but only for an instant and then through a fading fog.

Again he saw them, hurried ahead of them and waited. They re-appeared in the same postures of their leaving, were present for a bare instant, and then were gone again.

There were houses there the next "time," houses and people that got in his way; the next "time" again, there was a village, and then a small city was there.

But the returning group was slowing, and Ackerman saw that they were changing their posture a bit. The looks of anger and fear were dying; tenseness was leaving their bodies; they were turning to face one another.

It was upon the next "time" that Ackerman snapped his projector at them. He might as well have snapped his fingers; nothing happened.

He wondered, then smiled in frustration. How could he bring an object in from the other world that was not there? He could not; he could but wait until they returned and then grab them quick, again, before they had a chance to do any damage.

He raced forward quite a distance and looked them over. They were moving now, walking and talking to one another. Ackerman could not hear them for he was in his "time-ship" with the "lid" down for instant flight. He cursed the haze; it made a careful estimate of the instant of their arrival almost impossible. Especially now when they were beginning to blend in with the people of the "real world."

He saw it, then. They were idly walking, coming on the time-strata of solidity a full yard above the ground. Descending; walking through a Real World building toward a Real World sidewalk. They would meet—their Real World identities who were coming along the street in the same formation, talking in the same fashion.

Converging, wraith and ghost came together, passed through one another, approached a perfect register. Then as they blended into one being each, Ackerman gave a sharp cry and slammed down on his switch.

HE SAW IT again. They parted, wraiths from ghosts, and continued on their respective paths. The group in the Real World continued along the street, talking animatedly. The others—solid to Ackerman and themselves, stopped in baffled amazement.

They saw his car, and him. "What is this?" demanded Barry Ford. "Where did you come from? And how in the name of the Seven Deadly Sins do we seem to be walking—wading, so help me—ankle deep in the ground?"

Ackerman sat down in utter weariness. He had done it, all right. He had brought them! He had split the instant on the instant, and with this result.

In the world of Reality, Barry and Louis Ford, and Joan and Tod Laplane were free to go and tell all. In his world of time-space, Les Ackerman had four completely baffled people who would never have known of time-space and the split worlds if he, Ackerman, had not interfered.

He had wondered about the destruction of Calvin Blaine's world, had sent Blaine off to find his—Ackerman's—own previous "time-self" because it had been Ackerman's opinion that the destruction of Calvin Blaine's world only be obtained in a situation where the Laplane-Ford group had been returned. That, he believed, was a transitory situation that would be averted as soon as he caught up with them.

Then came the next blaze of mental lightning. Calvin Blaine was no man's fool; knowing that Ackerman must release the other group after meeting Calvin for the first time. Blaine would also know that when he interrupted the love scene, it would be Ackerman's first knowledge of Calvin Blaine.

Then. Right then. If Calvin and Laurie Blaine permitted themselves to be caught up with the so-called "edge of time-space" with Lester Ackerman, the latter would never meet the Laplane-Ford group.

There would be no telling, no information, and hence no strife. That of itself would be fine. But the twin worlds would eventually come together, both in "space" and in "time," and trouble would ensue from that alone. He, Ackerman, was the only man who could do something about that.

Quickly, he brought the group before him up to date. He told them as much as he could, told them to go and meet the Blaines, who were trying to get lost through the edge of the "time-split." It took some telling, some explanation, and quite a bit of convincing.

Eventually, they agreed. "But how will we go?" asked Barry Ford.

Ackerman wondered, and then grinned. "Simple; I'll not wait long. For I shall send the next person I meet in "time" to this instant to meet me. In fact," he said with genuine amusement, "I may send myself. And here I come now—see?"

The other car was sliding down, solidifying rapidly as it came into the time-space instant of Ackerman's unreal "present."

"We—"

"Get going," said Les. "I want to talk to myself in peace and quiet." They left, and Ackerman went to the other car, which had landed.

THE DRIVER was a stranger. He was about Ackerman's size and build, perhaps a little less gaunt and strained. He had a certain grim humor—sardonic, but still compassionate.

He stepped from the car and faced Ackerman. "So," he said with a sarcastic leer. "You are Lester Ackerman, The Great Physicist!"

"Now listen," snarled Ackerman angrily. "I don't—"

"Well, well!" laughed the other. "Look, Ackerman; for a Great Physicist, you are certainly making a sheer mess out of this."

"It's pretty much of a mess as it is!"

"Only what you've made it. You know, I should really let you stew in your own juice; it'll make a better man of you. It's only that I want to see you come through this at all that I interfere. Chum, you've boiled up a real tangle."

"I have?"

"This mess is of your making," insisted the stranger. "Shall I recount?"

"Please do," snapped Ackerman superciliously. "But after you tell me who you are."

"I happen to be Tansie Lee's husband."

"You—" stammered Ackerman. That, possibly, was the one thing that could—and did—fluster him completely. Not only that, but he showed it in every line of his body, every gesture, every stammering syllable. The other got a laugh out of Ackerman's complete loss of personal control.

"Don't apologize," he said. "I sent Tansie Lee; I hoped that you would be smart enough to figure it out with her help. You aren't."

"Did you instruct Tansie Lee to make love to me?"

"Tansie did nothing wrong," said the man. "What was wrong—completely, and totally—was your attitude."

Then he held up a hand as Ackerman was about to continue. "Not now," he said. "You've got to untangle this mess first."

"Go ahead," said Les. "Untangle."

"You," said Tansie Lee's husband, "were met by my wife in a state of ignorance concerning this fine mix-up. You were intercepted by the Blaines, whom you, yourself, sent recently to do the intercepting. You even gave them information that would best cause the breakup of intelligent understanding between Tansie and yourself. The Blaines reached you and intercepted. That fouled up my initial plans. Then you and the Blaines were intercepted again by the Laplane-Ford outfit—which you again sent to do the intercepting. Interestingly snarled, Ackerman; but when Barry Ford told you with such certainty that the Blaines were leading you to the instant of entrapped no-return at the so-called "edge of time-space," Barry Ford was merely echoing your own fears.

Fears which were installed in you, by the way, by Barry, who was recounting your own—oh Hell and Damnation!"

"Mind telling me where the Blaines come in?"

"Certainly. But I won't. You brought them."

"I'll be damned if I bring them."

The other man smiled knowingly. "As you tried to corral the other gang?"

"Meaning?" demanded Les.

"There's many's the slip. *'A would some power the giftie gi'e us, to see ourselves as ithers see us'* " quoted Tansie Lee's husband. "I suppose you're not to blame; but you will agree that it is quite a mess."

"Agreed. Now what do I do about it?"

"Ackerman, what started all this?"

"A strange explosion brought about by the Temperon metal in the cyclotron-set-up."

"And how is it to end?"

ACKERMAN sat down and put his face in his hands. "I don't know," he said soberly. "It seems that I am to make a choice between worlds. I can save one but not the other."

As Ackerman sat there, face lowered and spirits lower, he was in complete misery and totally oblivious to everything about him. One thing only penetrated the depth of his introversion.

That one thing was the cool touch of a soft hand on his shoulder. There was a delicate scent—one that brought memories, both delicately fond and angrily disconcerting. Tansie Lee seated herself beside him and put an arm over his shoulder. "Don't do that to him," she said, speaking to her husband with pleading.

"I can't live his life," he answered; "one more thing, and he'll be all right."

Ackerman looked from one to the other, puzzled. Had he been the other man, he would have been consumed with jealousy. "What?" he asked weakly.

"I can't tell you completely," said the other, "but it has to do with the "time-fission" and the Temperon. You'll figure it out."

It came to Ackerman that he *did* have the answer. The way to solve the problem was to use his ability to remove the Temperon from the cyclotron, and thus avert the explosion!

Tansie stood up. "Come on, Les," she said to him.

"Come on?" he asked dully.

"Yes," said her husband. "Finish what you started; you see, both Tansie and I have a rather large stake in this thing."

He turned and headed across the ground to a second time ship, entered, and left.

Ackerman stood up and shook his head nervously. "Well, Mrs. Lee," he said, and he mentally winced as he used her pet prefacing word.

She smiled, gamin-like, and said: "But I'm not Mrs. Lee. Tansie Lee is my given name. You see, Les, I am Mrs. Lester Ackerman!"

"You—but—uh—"

She laughed gurglingly. "That's another thing that is completely wrong with this time-space," she said; "right now I'm married to you but you aren't married to me. So if there's any question of convention, Lester, you are the guilty party, not I."

Ackerman sat back down again and groaned.

"But you just be a good, sensible boy," she promised coyly, "and someday you will be."

"So that was—me?" he asked in a strained voice.

She nodded.

"You mean to tell me that I didn't recognize myself?" he demanded.

Again she nodded. "You see, Les, you—and everybody—is used to seeing himself in a mirror. No face or person is symmetrical; that mole on your right cheek is always on your mirror image's left cheek—but it was still on the other Ackerman's right cheek. Also; you expected that if that ship did contain yourself, coming to get you as you so happily told the Ford-Laplane outfit, you expected that you would make some wisecrack about it. Therefore you didn't expect yourself to be coming as you did. Quite simple, I call it."

"Another angle on this mad tangle," said Les. "I'll be glad to get out of it."

"So will I," said Tansie.

"And I'm going to start right now!"

CHAPTER NINE

BELOW THEM lay the depressed green-glaze bowl of atomic horror; above stood the silent laboratory, deserted and awaiting the arrival of the technicians for the next morning's work.

Hazily in sight was the Temperon sample, and the radiation counters were clicking off at a fast rate.

"What are you going to do?" asked Tansie, in a voice that was filled with fear.

Ackerman stood up and stretched. "I am going to remove that sample," he said with an air of finality. "Then the time-fission will not take place, and there need be no ultimate conflict between the twin worlds."

"You mustn't," she breathed.

"No?"

"No," she told him. "For if you do, I shall not live, and we will never—" she let the sentence die.

He faced her squarely. "Tansie," he said, "It will be very easy for me to fall deeply in love with you. Given another day it could certainly be obtained. Yet the lives and desires of two people must not prevail to the death and destruction of a world full of people. Though it mean death to me, I could not live knowing that billions of people died because I was selfish."

Tansie looked at him tearfully.

"You'd sacrifice me?"

"You make it difficult," he said. "One life for a billion lives. And yet," he said, brightly, "you do exist; does that not prove something?"

"Only that in this world of probability and unreal existence, I am a definite probability."

"Yes," he told her. "This is the world of probability. I am not in the Real World, nor are you. If I do this, who is to tell me that we two may not go on forever in our own world of probability?"

"No," she said pleadingly. "Oh Les—I do so want—"

"I'll chance it," he said. "Because I must. I—look!"

Tansie turned. There, appearing with that thickening of the substance that characterized the arrival of a time car was the Blaines' ship. And beside it was the other one. Doors emerged, and the six got out of their ships and faced one another.

"So!" snapped Calvin Blaine. "We can finish this right here."

"Don't ask for mercy," snapped Barry Ford. "Nor expect sportsmanship. This is for keeps, and for the permanent existence of a whole world."

Tansie shuddered. "They'll fight," she said. "Because whichever side wins, they will prevent the others from returning to their worlds with the information that is needed. One and one alone will survive—and it is not fair, four to two, and Calvin Blaine an elderly man."

Tod Laplane lifted his gun; Laurie Blaine, her blonde hair a shining halo, pointed a revolver at Joan Laplane, who raced forward like a raven-haired fury, a gleaming knife in her hand. Barry Ford shook his broad shoulders and leaped—just as a shot rang out from the side.

They all turned. And across the space behind the Ford-Laplane ship there came another couple. A second Calvin and Laurie Blaine, armed.

In all, only four shots were fired before the embattled ones came to contact blows. Then the guns were wrested from fighting hands and it was tooth and nail.

"Come on," said Ackerman. "Because what you see is but eight people. If we do not, there will be that many billions of people fighting to the death."

Their motion caught eyes in the fighting crowd. Both sides were apparently wary of more reinforcements. None of them knew how many would be coming back; it is conceivable that whole armies could be built up of people returning to fight this battle.

But it was Les and Tansie Lee that they saw, and they stopped. Then Les and Tansie were in their ship, and Les was at the control board.

THE OTHER crowd boiled in, behind them, the fight forgotten, momentarily. They wanted Les Ackerman above all, for he was in a position to nullify any of their acts, regardless of which side won. He was not going to elude them again; they would continue this battle in Ackerman's presence so that the winner would be able to overpower the physicist.

Ackerman nudged the automatic controls. The time-space vehicle started forward in space and backwards in time.

Behind him the two factions eyed one another suspiciously, and moved warily to get into fighting-position.

Les turned briefly, and shook his head. Getting into that battle himself would be no good. *Let them fight!* he thought to himself. *Give me "time."* Ackerman could best win by removing the cause.

He flipped the top-hatch open and groped out of the moving ship with his gloved hand—the Temperon-coated glove—hoping to locate by sheer luck the cyclotron target and the Temperon sample, by luck aided with a good memory of where it was. He thought for a moment that he, himself, was not far from here in both "time" and "space." He was separated in space by the radiation-proof barrier, and in time only by the few instants of temporal fission.

Then he saw it! Vaguely, dimly, distorted by the gray-green haze that enveloped the ship in motion.

The ship stalled. It could not penetrate the barrier of "time" to head into the "past" which would have been previous to the fission of "time." So Ackerman nudged the power up higher and the temporal drive of the ship strained against the barrier like an automobile straining against an immobile wall.

Ackerman reached for the Temperon.

Tansie cried: "No, Les!" She ran to take his hands from the open hatch.

He took her by the shoulders and shook her gently. "You'll be all right," he said softly; "it is a chance we must take!"

"But—" she said uncertainly, and stopped because of the roar that came from behind.

"Ackerman!" bellowed Tod Laplane. "He's removing the original Temperon!"

"If he does!" swore Barry Ford, ""We'll not exist!"

Their private fight forgotten, both factions turned and hurled themselves at Ackerman.

Eight people to one—and Tansie Lee still against his purpose to boot; he shook her free and reached, missed, and tried again.

The roar of noise stopped. Ackerman caught it out of the corner of one eye. Tansie Lee still believed that the removal of the Temperon and the resulting correction of the time-split would make her non-existent, but she was standing there with a wicked-looking shotgun poised across one shapely hip. If she fired, the kick would turn her around, and Tansie knew it, for she was pointing the gun to her left. The second shot would sweep the right side of the room, and the chances were excellent that no one would be much alive after the third.

Limbo—the land of non-existence—might be her lot, but until she left here, no one was going to harm Les Ackerman.

He shook all thoughts from his mind and reached again. And this time he touched it!

THE GRAY-GREEN haze parted in a flare of light. Ackerman saw both the deuterium-ice target and the Temperon clearly; it was the latter that gave him pause.

For out from the Temperon sample was growing a shimmering, uncertain sphere of energy. It expanded and then hurled itself outward with lightning rapidity. Out it went, to the ends of the infinite universe.

Then destruction, sheer and complete, broke loose. The time-ship was hurled away, but not before they saw solid matter burst into a coruscation of incandescent gas, and flame up out of its wraithlike self into a pillar of boiling clouds that headed for the stratosphere. Below them, the ground seared upwards and sintered downwards and fused into an ugly gray-green glaze.

"So," said Ackerman, shaking with reaction. "So Lester Ackerman himself is the cause of the fission in "time." You may stop fighting, gentlemen. Tansie, you can stop pointing that cannon at them, too."

Calvin Blaine came forward and took it from her shaking hands. She turned blindly, like an automaton; then she looked up at Les and reality came once more across her face. "Les!" she cried and hurled herself forward into his arms.

Calvin turned to his other, time-separated self. "Please leave," he said. "This is most disconcerting."

One Laurie Blaine shrugged at the other. "I don't even like myself as competition," she said.

One pair of Blaines left the ship; the other Calvin Blaine looked out of the window and chuckled. "They left," he said, "just in time to get into that fight!"

"Then this," replied his daughter, "is the ship they came in!"

"Ours is over there," said Blaine; "let's go."

"But what about them—and him?" asked Laurie indicating the others in Ackerman's ship.

"I think," said Blaine, "that nothing we do can change much right now. Ackerman himself is the one that must be moving next."

Barry Ford grunted angrily. It was quite apparent that a sudden thought had occurred to him. He herded his friends out and into their own ship.

"Hell!" said Blaine, taking Laurie by the arm and almost hurling her out.

"What's got into them?" asked Tansie.

"It has occurred to them that there is one more very definite danger for them all. They've got to go there to prevent it. Foolishly, they're hurrying when they know that I've got a lot of work to do first, and still will end up where they are at the proper instant."

"Work?" asked Tansie.

"Uh-huh," he said. "I've some correcting to do. Will you drive us along the Blaines' side of this Time-stream, I'm going to peck at the typewriter a bit."

*　*　*

IT WAS a long time later. Ackerman had written several thousand words on the subject, and was now peering through one of the ship windows at the laboratory through which the time-space ship was parked. Then, satisfied, he nodded.

"Push here," he said cryptically.

"Huh?" asked Tansie.

"Part of my corrective work," he said. "So help me, I started this mess; I'm going to be the one that cleans it up."

He used the projector to drag a few odd items into the "time-space" from the "real world" laboratory.

"On the other side of that barrier," he told Tansie, "there are a couple of characters bootlegging a bit of private research."

"What are you going to do?"

"They are going to have themselves a high-grade atomic explosion."

"Won't that be dangerous? And how will it cause corrective measures?"

Les grinned with self-satisfaction. "This," he said waving his hands, "is the world of throttled research. Like all times of prohibition, there are people who will bootleg, whether it be liquor, dope, or knowledge. This explosion, however, will do two things to that world. They will understand that there are a lot of people doing the same thing—and will also know that this same thing might happen again and again, because no one has the faintest idea of what anybody else is doing! When the first chemist mixed gunpowder, he was able to warn other chemists not to mix more than so much—or else. But after this atomic blowup, no one will be able to do any warning—and they'll not know what line of research these people were taking."

"Yes," said Tansie uncertainly.

"Then, in order to bring it all out in the clear and the open, they must repeal their laws that throttle and forbid research. This will make Blaine's world less divergent."

He reached forward with his Temperon-clad glove and took firm hold of the Temperon sample in the "Real" world cyclotron.

During the boiling, coruscating roar of the atomic hell, Tansie held her breath. The ship was driven away before she spoke.

"Temperon again," she said. "Isn't that likely to cause another time-split?"

He shook his head. "No," he said. "Time splits only when there is two very definite possibilities for a future. Individual and minute acts such as might be called a major catastrophe on earth do nothing to disturb the 'temporal' advance. You see, Tansie, Man is an animal possessing free will, and he can do as he pleases. But his every act is based upon his past experience, and therefore whatever he does is reasonably predictable. Therefore, while it is possible to state that a tree might grow in two possible ways, the fact is that it grows only one way and therefore we have no multiplicity of worlds of probability. There is no Wheel of If."

CHAPTER TEN

"BUT WHAT about the people who were running that thing?" asked Tansie.

"Tough," said Ackerman. "But better them than—"

"No," said Tansie, taking his arm and shaking it pleadingly. "Not murder, Les."

"Okay," he said. "But you are making me a lot of trouble. By insisting, I mean."

"How?"

"Watch," he said. He drove the time-space ship back towards the "past" and stopped it previous to the explosion. He plied the projector in the operating chamber of the cyclotron, and two people solidified and came to the unreal world. "Meet Calvin and Laurie Blaine," said Ackerman.

Tansie gulped and sat down hard. Calvin Blaine blinked and said: "How did this come to be?"

Ackerman shook his head tiredly.

He handed Blaine the several sheets of typescript. "Here," he said. "This gives you enough information for a beginning. Once you grasp the situation, you are to do the job outlined on the last four pages."

He turned to Tansie. "Drive the ship to Barry Ford's world, while I try to explain what's to be done."

"What are you going to do?" she asked him.

"There are some strings still untied," smiled Ackerman, who was now master of the situation and worthy of the name of Great Physicist. "The Blaines are going to build me my laboratory!"

He left Calvin and Laurie in the familiar woods of Wisconsin on the other world, complete with his projector and the plans. Then down through the "time-space" he and Tansie went, on that world, to an era that Ackerman knew to be the critical "time."

"We 'pushed' there," he said. "Now we 'pry' here."

"What kind of measure comes here?"

"Same prescription," said Ackerman, reaching for his Temperon-clad glove.

"And is this where the Ford-Laplane outfit comes in?"

"No. Since this is the world of free research, the cyclotron laboratory will be remotely controlled and unattended. No one will get hurt."

"But I don't understand how the same cure works on both worlds," complained Tansie.

"Very simple. The other world didn't know what one another was doing because everybody was afraid to talk. In this world no one knows what his neighbor is doing because, with everybody doing it, there is too little correlation of effort. No one has to ask anybody's permission to tinker, and so when this laboratory goes up, again no one will be quite sure of what caused it."

"But those who were running it will," objected Tansie.

Ackerman smiled. "Tansie Lee is one of my favorite cooks," he told her. "She's been cooking for years. And would Tansie know what happened if she mixed up a batch of baking powder biscuits out of her grandmother's old tried and true recipe—used in the family for years—and when she popped them in the oven to cook, they exploded and destroyed the end of the house?"

"So?" she smiled. "You're going to take a standard experiment and fudge it up?"

"Yup," he said with a grin, waving a bit of Temperon, held in his Temperon-clad glove.

Again the explosion boiled skyward, and the flame and the blast seared the eyeballs and battered at the eardrums. Then it was over, and they were gone again.

"And now?" asked Tansie.

"Now we effect the coalescence of two worlds of probability," he told her.

*   *   *

LES ACKERMAN drove the time-space vehicle at a headlong pace into the future. He nodded with satisfaction when he noted that the destruction of Calvin Blaine's world was not to be. And though he had never seen the opposing success in probability—the destruction of the world of free research—he knew about when its probable destruction took place. He watched, and was gratified to know that his acts had averted the successful culmination of either side's plans for conquest.

On through time-space went Ackerman and Tansie Lee, across the years until it was apparent that the twin worlds of dual probability were, indeed, coming closer together. For as Les explained it, when the world of throttled research opened up, and the world of too-free research closed down, they began to become more and more like one another. So they were coming closer together not only in attitude, but in "space" as well.

Slowly and ponderously they came together. It took years from the initial tangential contact to where their surfaces were almost in perfect register.

And Ackerman sought through the doubled-world again and found running the time-space vehicle difficult because the congruency of the two worlds made through-passage impossible. But across the world he went, even so.

And he found what he was looking for. In both worlds, men were working on research problems. It was a crazy scene; the laboratories were in excellent register, and appeared as one. The men, of course, were free to move, and they were not performing the same acts. It made for a blurring, maddening scene to watch men working furiously in a large laboratory and working through one another.

Then one man in each world turned from his work and held up a sample. They were about eight feet apart in space.

Their fellows stopped work also, and each group went below.

"Now," said Ackerman, "if we're lucky—"

"This," said Tansie Lee, "is where we part."

"Part?" he asked in wonder.

She nodded. "I am going back—to you—my husband. After all, Lester, we have yet to meet for the truly first time. That is—well—I mean I can't very well marry you twice in "time," you know. You'll have to make the acquaintance of Tansie Lee for the first time, too."

"When do we part?"

"As soon as you are successful."

"I'll be looking for you," he said. Then he stopped short, standing in the hallway of the laboratory as the men trouped past—through—the two of them on their way to the cyclotron chamber below.

He took her by the shoulders and turned her to face him. "I can kiss a married woman," he said, "with a free mind so long as she is married to me."

She went into his arms to be held—as she was holding him—close. Ackerman more than half expected another interruption, but it did not come. That annoying thought faded as he found his entire attention held by the softly eager woman in his arms. Long, tender, silent moments passed, and then returned reality.

"I like your looks," he told her. "And that was a temporary goodbye. I'll be most careful not to make any mistakes."

Tansie's eyes were shining brightly but she merely nodded and said only: "Auf wiedersehen, my darling."

ACKERMAN turned and hurried down the laboratory steps with Tansie behind him. They arrived just as both technicians were placing the samples to be bombarded in the cyclotron—one in each world but in perfect register. Ackerman stood in the room beside the big machine as the others left, his Temperon-clad glove poised over the congruent samples.

Then and only then he saw the rest. They came hurriedly, fearfully. But not in hatred of one another.

Calvin Blaine shook his head. "You should not have done this," he said.

"But it is done," added Barry Ford. "Now he must have perfect coordination, or else."

Tod Laplane shrugged. "If he coalesces these twin worlds at the wrong 'time', there will be the damndest celestially cosmic explosion since the beginning of the universe."

Louis Ford said: "Maybe that's how the universe really started."

Laurie Blaine shook her head. "Don't be a pessimist," she said. Then she turned to Ackerman with pleading eyes. "Please be careful," she said. "After all, you haven't met Tansie Lee yet; and I am your woman, Lester."

Joan Laplane, as attractively dark as Laurie Blaine was beautifully blonde, stood beside the other girl. There was no sign of scorn, nor even embarrassment between them, and she added her bit to the moment: "You'd not destroy a world for the love of a woman, Lester. That's commendable. I've not mentioned how I felt because of reasons known to both of us. But," she said to Ackerman, but facing both Tansie Lee and Laurie Blaine, "until Lester places a wedding ring on some girl's finger, I'm considering myself as active competition."

Tansie laughed confidently. "Dream on," she said, "but remember, I'm the one he'll marry."

"That's only a good probability, said Laurie. "But no certain thing."

"Shut up," said Calvin Blaine. "This is no time to get his nerves on edge, Ackerman. Don't do it. Let these worlds diverge again, and go on whole."

Ackerman shook his head. "Can't be done," he said.

Then the cyclotron started beside him, and a stream of bluish haze surrounded the target and the sample. Ackerman timed it, and then clamped his hand down hard on the bit of Temperon in the machine…

*   *   *

THERE WAS a solid wave of sound, and a torrent of sheer energy that stormed at them. The earth shook in a series of abrupt shocks, and from somewhere there converged a film of shimmering something that marked the boundary of a field of energetic force. It came closing in, and disappeared within the bit of Temperon. That much Ackerman saw before he blacked-out completely, shaken with pain.

But this was no atomic explosion. Instead of sending the laboratory skyward in a billowing cloud of energetic particles, the force of the blast was confined to the space within the cyclotron room.

And then the energy that was compressed by the spherical shell was driven into the "past"—into the era of "fissioned-time." That period needed that cosmic energy in order to function at all.

The cycle was ended, the story finished. Ackerman had started the fission, and had effected its end.

The cyclotron workers, all unknowing, had coalesced; had become a single probability again. They entered, and found Ackerman lying there.

It never was explained to their satisfaction. Nor could they understand why and how he managed to be in the cyclotron chamber during a bombardment without getting badly irradiated. Ackerman accepted their help and their solace for his aches, but said no more.

He started to leave the laboratory, and he was very thoughtful. He alone of them all was here. The Fords, Laplanes, and Blaines were all gone inexplicably—possibly back into the realm of unreal time. That meant that the Blaines went back to their laboratory to be—

Not necessarily. Forewarned is forearmed and Ackerman had no proof that they were in the explosion. They could not stop the blow-up, but they could, and probably would, leave for safety so soon as the time-conservation-energy factor returned them.

But even so, Ackerman was sorry. Sorry, and yet glad. For his possible woman-trouble had gone along with the trouble with the time-split.

He looked out of the door and saw—

Tansie Lee!

"Tansie!" be shouted.

HE RAN—and crashed through the glass of the door, landed on the sidewalk in a welter of broken glass. She turned. "Impulsive, aren't you?"

"Tansie!" he breathed, reaching for her hands.

"That is my name," she said. "But who are you?"

"Les Ackerman," he told her. "And you'll be seeing a lot of me!"

She smiled. "Come and tell me about it," she said. She looked up at him leadingly—and for the first time, Lester Ackerman noticed that her eyes were as blue as any blonde's—Laurie's, for instance, but her complexion was definitely brunette, as dark as Joan's. Her auburn hair was—halfway between.

He linked arms with her. "This," he said, "is probably the best of all probable worlds."

EPILOGUE

The woman moved from her husband's arms and faced the vehicle with distaste. "I hate to go," she said.

"You must," he told her. "And quickly, or there will not be enough power to penetrate the 'Real World' back to the 'fissioned-time'. I'd send someone else, but no one but you and I can go through 'time' to the dual worlds."

She nodded unhappily, and started the machine. It disappeared instantly, leaping the "time" between now and the "time" of fissioned probability, where such a machine could easily function. It was back immediately, and she hurled herself tearfully into her husband's arms.

"I've muffed it terribly," she sobbed.

He stroked her head, and then seated her on the ground beside the machine. He got in, disappeared, and also returned instantly.

"There," he told her. "And that is that."

He lifted her from the ground, put his arm about her lissome waist, and walked her to the house, leaving the machine.

Tomorrow he would dismantle it. It was the only one of its kind, and its usefulness was over. Finished, washed-up, obsolete. After a total Real Operating Time of less than ten milliseconds.

But during which time it had really been around!

THE END

If you've enjoyed this book, you will not want to miss these terrific titles…

ARMCHAIR SCI-FI & HORROR DOUBLE NOVELS, $12.95 each

D-1 **THE GALAXY RAIDERS** by William P. McGivern
SPACE STATION #1 by Frank Belknap Long

D-2 **THE PROGRAMMED PEOPLE** by Jack Sharkey
SLAVES OF THE CRYSTAL BRAIN by William Carter Sawtelle

D-3 **YOU'RE ALL ALONE** by Fritz Leiber
THE LIQUID MAN by Bernard C. Gilford

D-4 **CITADEL OF THE STAR LORDS** by Edmond Hamilton
VOYAGE TO ETERNITY by Milton Lesser

D-5 **IRON MEN OF VENUS** by Don Wilcox
THE MAN WITH ABSOLUTE MOTION by Noel Loomis

D-6 **WHO SOWS THE WIND…** by Rog Phillips
THE PUZZLE PLANET by Robert A. W. Lowndes

D-7 **PLANET OF DREAD** by Murray Leinster
TWICE UPON A TIME by Charles L. Fontenay

D-8 **THE TERROR OUT OF SPACE** by Dwight V. Swain
QUEST OF THE GOLDEN APE by Ivar Jorgensen and Adam Chase

D-9 **SECRET OF MARRACOTT DEEP** by Henry Slesar
PAWN OF THE BLACK FLEET by Mark Clifton.

D-10 **BEYOND THE RINGS OF SATURN** by Robert Moore Williams
A MAN OBSESSED by Alan E. Nourse

ARMCHAIR SCIENCE FICTION CLASSICS, $12.95 each

C-1 **THE GREEN MAN**
by Harold M. Sherman

C-2 **A TRACE OF MEMORY**
By Keith Laumer

C-3 **INTO PLUTONIAN DEPTHS**
by Stanton A. Coblentz

ARMCHAIR MASTERS OF SCIENCE FICTION SERIES, $16.95 each

M-1 **MASTERS OF SCIENCE FICTION, Vol. One**
Bryce Walton—"Dark of the Moon" and other tales

M-2 **MASTERS OF SCIENCE FICTION, Vol. Two**
Jerome Bixby—"One Way Street" and other tales

If you've enjoyed this book, you will not want to miss these terrific titles…

ARMCHAIR SCI-FI & HORROR DOUBLE NOVELS, $12.95 each

D-21   **EMPIRE OF EVIL** by Robert Arnette
THE SIGN OF THE TIGER by Alan E. Nourse & J. A. Meyer

D-22   **OPERATION SQUARE PEG** by Frank Belknap Long
ENCHANTRESS OF VENUS by Leigh Brackett

D-23   **THE LIFE WATCH** by Lester del Rey
CREATURES OF THE ABYSS by Murray Leinster

D-24   **LEGION OF LAZARUS** by Edmond Hamilton
STAR HUNTER by Andre Norton

D-25   **EMPIRE OF WOMEN** by John Fletcher
ONE OF OUR CITIES IS MISSING by Irving Cox

D-26   **THE WRONG SIDE OF PARADISE** by Raymond F. Jones
THE INVOLUNTARY IMMORTALS by Rog Phillips

D-27   **EARTH QUARTER** by Damon Knight
ENVOY TO NEW WORLDS by Keith Laumer

D-28   **SLAVES TO THE METAL HORDE** by Milton Lesser
HUNTERS OUT OF TIME by Joseph E. Kelleam

D-29   **RX JUPITER SAVE US** by Ward Moore
BEWARE THE USURPERS by Geoff St. Reynard

D-30   **SECRET OF THE SERPENT** by Don Wilcox
CRUSADE ACROSS THE VOID by Dwight V. Swain

ARMCHAIR SCIENCE FICTION CLASSICS, $12.95 each

C-7   **THE SHAVER MYSTERY, Book One**
by Richard S. Shaver

C-8   **THE SHAVER MYSTERY, Book Two**
by Richard S. Shaver

C-9   **MURDER IN SPACE**
by David V. Reed

ARMCHAIR MASTERS OF SCIENCE FICTION SERIES, $16.95 each

M-3   **MASTERS OF SCIENCE FICTION, Vol. Three**
Robert Sheckley, "The Perfect Woman" and other tales

M-4   **MASTERS OF SCIENCE FICTION, Vol. Four**
Mack Reynolds, Part One, "Stowaway" and other tales

If you've enjoyed this book, you will not want to miss these terrific titles…

ARMCHAIR SCI-FI & HORROR DOUBLE NOVELS, $12.95 each

D-31   **A HOAX IN TIME** by Keith Laumer
         INSIDE EARTH by Poul Anderson

D-32   **TERROR STATION** by Dwight V. Swain
         THE WEAPON FROM ETERNITY by Dwight V. Swain

D-33   **THE SHIP FROM INFINITY** by Edmond Hamilton
         TAKEOFF by C. M. Kornbluth

D-34   **THE METAL DOOM** by David H. Keller
         TWELVE TIMES ZERO by Howard Browne

D-35   **HUNTERS OUT OF SPACE** by Joseph Kelleam
         INVASION FROM THE DEEP by Paul W. Fairman,

D-36   **THE BEES OF DEATH** by Robert Moore Williams
         A PLAGUE OF PYTHONS by Frederik Pohl

D-37   **THE LORDS OF QUARMALL** by Fritz Leiber and Harry Fischer
         BEACON TO ELSEWHERE by James H. Schmitz

D-38   **BEYOND PLUTO** by John S. Campbell
         ARTERY OF FIRE by Thomas N. Scortia

D-39   **SPECIAL DELIVERY** by Kris Neville
         NO TIME FOR TOFFEE by Charles F. Meyers

D-40   **JUNGLE IN THE SKY** by Milton Lesser
         RECALLED TO LIFE by Robert Silverberg

ARMCHAIR SCIENCE FICTION CLASSICS, $12.95 each

C-10   **MARS IS MY DESTINATION**
         by Frank Belknap Long

C-11   **SPACE PLAGUE**
         by George O. Smith

C-12   **SO SHALL YE REAP**
         by Rog Phillips

ARMCHAIR SCI-FI & HORROR GEMS SERIES, $12.95 each

G-3   **SCIENCE FICTION GEMS, Vol. Two**
         James Blish and others

G-4   **HORROR GEMS, Vol. Two**
         Joseph Payne Brennan and others

If you've enjoyed this book, you will not want to miss these terrific titles…

ARMCHAIR SCI-FI & HORROR DOUBLE NOVELS, $12.95 each

D-81   **THE LAST PLEA** by Robert Bloch
          THE STATUS CIVILIZATION by Robert Sheckley

D-82   **WOMAN FROM ANOTHER PLANET** by Frank Belknap Long
          HOMECALLING by Judith Merril

D-83   **WHEN TWO WORLDS MEET** by Robert Moore Williams
          THE MAN WHO HAD NO BRAINS by Jeff Sutton

D-84   **THE SPECTRE OF SUICIDE SWAMP** by E. K. Jarvis
          IT'S MAGIC, YOU DOPE! by Jack Sharkey

D-85   **THE STARSHIP FROM SIRIUS** by Rog Phillips
          FINAL WEAPON by Everett Cole

D-86   **TREASURE ON THUNDER MOON** by Edmond Hamilton
          TRAIL OF THE ASTROGAR by Henry Haase

D-87   **THE VENUS ENIGMA** by Joe Gibson
          THE WOMAN IN SKIN 13 by Paul W. Fairman

D-88   **THE MAD ROBOT** by William P. McGivern
          THE RUNNING MAN by J. Holly Hunter

D-89   **VENGEANCE OF KYVOR** by Randall Garrett
          AT THE EARTH'S CORE by Edgar Rice Burroughs

D-90   **DWELLERS OF THE DEEP** by Don Wilcox
          NIGHT OF THE LONG KNIVES by Fritz Leiber

ARMCHAIR SCIENCE FICTION CLASSICS, $12.95 each

C-28   **THE MAN FROM TOMORROW**
          by Stanton A. Coblentz

C-29   **THE GREEN MAN OF GRAYPEC**
          by Festus Pragnell

C-30   **THE SHAVER MYSTERY, Book Four**
          by Richard S. Shaver

ARMCHAIR MASTERS OF SCIENCE FICTION SERIES, $16.95 each

MS-7   **MASTERS OF SCIENCE FICTION AND FANTASY, Vol. Seven**
          Lester del Rey, "The Band Played On" and other tales

MS-8   **MASTERS OF SCIENCE FICTION, Vol. Eight**
          Milton Lesser, "'A' as in Android" and other tales

If you've enjoyed this book, you will not want to miss these terrific titles...

ARMCHAIR SCI-FI & HORROR DOUBLE NOVELS, $12.95 each

D-91   **THE TIME TRAP** by Henry Kuttner
         THE LUNAR LICHEN by Hal Clement

D-92   **SARGASSO OF LOST STARSHIPS** by Poul Anderson
         THE ICE QUEEN by Don Wilcox

D-93   **THE PRINCE OF SPACE** by Jack Williamson
         POWER by Harl Vincent

D-94   **PLANET OF NO RETURN** by Howard Browne
         THE ANNIHILATOR COMES by Ed Earl Repp

D-95   **THE SINISTER INVASION** by Edmond Hamilton
         OPERATION TERROR by Murray Leinster

D-96   **TRANSIENT** by Ward Moore
         THE WORLD-MOVER by George O. Smith

D-97   **FORTY DAYS HAS SEPTEMBER** by Milton Lesser
         THE DEVIL'S PLANET by David Wright O'Brien

D-98   **THE CYBERENE** by Rog Phillips
         BADGE OF INFAMY by Lester del Rey

D-99   **THE JUSTICE OF MARTIN BRAND** by Raymond A. Palmer
         BRING BACK MY BRAIN by Dwight V. Swain

D-100 **WIDE-OPEN PLANET** by L. Sprague de Camp
         AND THEN THE TOWN TOOK OFF by Richard Wilson

ARMCHAIR SCIENCE FICTION CLASSICS, $12.95 each

C-31   **THE GOLDEN GUARDSMEN**
         by S. J. Byrne

C-32   **ONE AGAINST THE MOON**
         by Donald A. Wollheim

C-33   **HIDDEN CITY**
         by Chester S. Geier

ARMCHAIR SCI-FI & HORROR GEMS SERIES, $12.95 each

G-9   **SCIENCE FICTION GEMS, Vol. Five**
         Clifford D. Simak and others

G-10   **HORROR GEMS, Vol. Five**
         E. Hoffman Price and others